Aliens from outer space don't exist
and that really pisses them off.

# The Truth about UFOs, Aliens and all that

By

# John Stanton

Gabriel's Horn Publishers
2009
www.nightwritersbooks.com

# Chapter 1

## The Mr. Hiemer Incident

Tina was sitting in her favorite Italian café but it really wasn't an Italian café. There was some Italian food on the menu but there were also hamburgers and gyros. The 'Kasbah Café' was decorated with Italian style stucco and the tables had red checkered table clothes with candles stuck in wine bottles. It looked Italian at first glance but the wine bottles were from French wines and the waiters wore black berets. It was all a weird mix of Euro-Middle-Eastern cuisine but if Tina squinted her eyes just right to blur her vision she could imagine she was in Venice, Italy.

Tina was pulled back to reality by Cassie's splashy celebrity entrance at the valet with her sparkling cherry red sports car, late as usual. She shook her head at the sight of Cassie sweeping in dressed like a fashion model always late for anything not related to her real estate business. She had told Cassie specifically to dress down for the evening but Cassie was dressed for a million dollar deal in a three piece suit sharpened by her long black hair pulled back tight into a bun on a bun.

"Sorry I'm late, my pitch ran long," Cassie said hustling up to the table still digging into her expensive leather purse to situate her car keys. "Have you been waiting long?"

"Not long ... You said six o'clock but I know that means six fifteen ..." Tina clucked her lips looking over

2

Cassie's outfit. "Girl friend, I told you dress casual. We were supposed to relax tonight and I was going to teach you how to really shoot pool," she said tossing her hair indignantly. Tina's bouncy red curls fell around her shoulders and could work with an evening gown or blue jeans. It matched her bright red lipstick and contrasted with fair white skin.

"Well, I just came from work," Cassie said embarrassed at thought of showing up at the neighborhood pool hall in her designer business suit. She really wouldn't care about her appearance but you never knew who could be a potential customer. "I think I've got some warm ups in the trunk of my car," she thought aloud.

"Warm Ups!" Tina said aghast at how Cassie could be so in-charge of the world then suddenly so out of touch with the world. "Are you nuts? There'll be men there, including a lot of military hunks from the base in full dress uniform! We're going back to my place. I got plenty of

3

stuff for you to wear," Tina announced resolutely with another toss of her red curls. "You know that any woman who only owns three piece suits is single and is going to stay that way."

Cassie was about to protest but her cell phone started ringing in her purse calling her back to the world of her career. She answered it then listened for a moment before she said, "Yes officer, what's the problem?"

Tina perked up like a Christmas tree that had just been plugged in when she heard the word, 'officer'. She leaned over and tried to listen to the cryptic conversation.

"Well, yes sir ... I haven't had any problems reported sir but ... Okay, I'll be right there," Cassie put away her cell phone still looking puzzled over the call. It was strange for her to be caught off guard by anything.

"Well?" Tina asked enthusiastically. She was always interested in juicy gossip about other people's business with the police. "What's going on?"

4

"You know the property I rent to that old man on Morningwood Street." Cassie was still trying to understand the situation as she explained it. "That little old man is on the roof of that house and the police can't get him to come down."

"What's he on some kind of protest or something?" Tina asked, her imagination reeling with the story of the old man on the roof.

"I don't know. They say he's flipping out." Cassie's eyes sank as she realized their evening was over before it began. For once, she had actually planned for a night off. "I'm sorry; I have to go check it out."

"Do you think they'll use rubber bullets on him or maybe tear gas?" Tina asked excitedly bouncing in her chair a little. "Oh wait! Can I go? They might use that big net thing on him! Oh! I want to go!" Tina loved this sort of thing.

"Would you go with me? I've had a long day and I could use all the help I can get." Cassie almost sounded pleading beset by the trials of her workday. Tina could always help even when she was no help at all.

"Oh yeah, I saw this stuff on TV that the cops use on rioters and protesters." Tina's enthusiasm for her own stories often drew others deep into them. "It's like a big fire hose cannon thing that shoots thick glue that coats people and holds them down. That could bring the old dude down!"

Cassie had to shake her head to escape Tina's story and the image of the old man immobilized in a blob of glue. They left together for Cassie's car, a classic red Jaguar coupe impeccably cleaned and waxed. As they drove away neither noticed a tall man with a pointed goatee and round wire frame glasses sitting alone at a table watching them from across the crowded patio.

"Why is this Mr. Hiemer this way?" Cassie asked to the sky as she drove through the suburbs. She felt like everyone she had talked to in the last week had been working against her to isolate her and orchestrate her life to keep her alone. "Why do old men get crazy and do things like this so that I have to drive out here? I've got a huge stack of paperwork at home. I've got city councilmen and county commissioners that keep trying to look down my dress and now the sheriff calls me." Suddenly, she realized she was supposed to be off of work then added, "... and we were supposed to go out."

Tina was sitting next to her in the passenger seat buffing her nails with some manicurist tool she pulled from her oversized purse. She shrugged her shoulders at first but could never resist a chance to give her opinion. "He's just a lonely old man and they pull this kind of shit all the time. Lonely old women get crazy too but they just sit around and collect cats." Something clicked in Tina's head and

7

she popped up with, "Hey that's it! You should get yourself a cat!"

"Oh so now I'm a lonely old woman." Cassie said rolling her eyes. The drive didn't demand much of her attention but Tina's remark about her lifestyle did. She heard it from Tina all the time. "Am I to the point now where I should collect cats?" Cassie asked with a grump.

"Well, you know I worry about you? I mean ... You haven't had a date in months, not since that Raymond guy and that's been almost a year ago. You're working a thousand hours a week since you picked up those two new properties and now you're having these nightmares. What's that all about?" Tina said almost breaking into chatter. She had known Cassie long enough to know how intense she was about work but in the years since Cassie's mother died it had become almost obsessive. Now Tina was really worried.

"Look I know you care and I love you for it," Cassie said. "But I just need some time off. Once I finish this SMS deal I'll take a vacation." She really did appreciate Tina's concern but felt pressured by it and just the idea of spending a week far from home made Cassie nervous. In fact, she really didn't like traveling. She was afraid of airplanes, and trains made her feel claustrophobic. Besides, the simple reality was that a workaholic life was just the price of success and Cassie didn't have to look past that.

"That's what you said before your last deal and the deal before that," Tina said insistently. She was always trying to talk Cassie into taking a Caribbean cruise on a luxury liner with her for a week of pampering. "Each time you pick up another rental property you're making more work."

"And more money!" Cassie interrupted another chatter burst. "Paid for this Jag we're riding in. Whenever the work starts to get to me, I come out and run my hand over the leather upholstery."

"Yeah, well how long will it be before you go nuts and the cops have to get you off the roof of your house like this Mr. Hiemer?" Tina wasn't even going to try to take on an argument of unabashed materialism with Cassie. It was best to change the subject. "You know when it happens I'll be there for you," Tina added lovingly.

"Thanks for coming with me on this one, T. Bartenders are supposed to be good at dealing with problem people." Cassie's persecuted feeling which had been building all week seeped to the surface. "I mean, I really am a good landlord, you know how hard I work and Mister Hiemer's really a nice old guy."

"Don't miss your turn!" Tina piped.

"I see it!" Cassie turned left onto Morningwood Street and had to slow down. She didn't know what to think about what she saw and it left her mind in an unexplored world she'd seen on TV. The scene they drove up on was the typical media circus cliché. A news van had already arrived and had its small dish antenna up sending signals. There was a fire truck with a hook and ladder team. Two police cars from the sheriff's department, two from the city police and an ambulance jammed the quiet neighborhood street. She wasn't sure why the tow truck was there but the lights on top of it were flashing like everything else parked around the house.

"Whoa! Cass, look at all this!" Tina marveled at the spectacle as Cassie negotiated the drive through the traffic jam. "This is better than the time my drunken brother-in-law drove his Winnebago off the ferry into the harbor. He got to ride in a helicopter when they picked him up out of the water. His Winnebago floated there for a while but they needed cranes and tugboats to move it. He didn't want it back so they just pulled it out of the way of ship traffic and let it sink," Tina reported in a verbal burst.

Cassie drove as close as they could get to the melee before they had to get out and walk through a scatter of parked emergency vehicles.  They approached the front

yard of the house that Cassie owned and old Stanley

Hiemer rented as its first and only tenant all these years.  It

was the third property she had bought and it reminded her

of a time when she finally considered herself a property

executive with a career.  It was an excitement that was

somehow lost with the years and not recaptured by the

money earned.

The police were holding back a crowd of onlookers

gathered for something visually spectacular.  Mr. Hiemer

had made serious and tempting offers to buy the property

many times saying that his potted rubber tree plant had

established a relationship with the other bushes in the yard

and he could never move away.  Cassie always knew he

was a little crazy but now above it all, squirming out on top

of a second story gable from the steep roof was old Mr.

Hiemer.  He straddled the gable precariously clutching

something to his chest and waving a roll of aluminum foil

at the crowd. The firemen had set up a big square airbag on the ground in front of the house just in case the man fell down the roof. They had to keep chasing kids away who were trying to crawl up and bounce on it.

Cassie and Tina wandered up to the unreal scene slack jawed. A stern deputy stopped them like he was directing a presidential motorcade so Cassie told the officer who she was and asked what happened.

"Well, he's been makin' trouble for the last few days," the deputy recited like he was reading a report. "Called the sheriff a couple of times this week sayin' space aliens are after him and this time we came out and found him on the roof. He says they took him up in a space ship just like in that movie." The officer had been all business until he got to this part of the story. He leaned closer and lowered his voice looking over the tops of his mirrored sunglasses. "says they gave him a rectal probe!"

"I don't believe this," Cassie said as she threw up her arms. "Why, out of the blue, flying saucers? Why's he on the roof with foil and whatever he's got?"

"Frosting!" Tina said.

Cassie and the deputy both looked at Tina.

"He's got a can of cake frosting. You know that ready made cake frosting in a can," Tina explained and pointed. "See the red logo ... that's my brand. You can eat it right out of the can. It's so good!"

"Look, forget this! Can I talk to him?" Cassie asked the deputy. "I've known this old man for years. I might be able to bring him back to reality."

"Well ... The FBI hostage negotiator won't be here for a few hours ... Let me ask the boss." The deputy consulted with the other authorities who had been discussing the option of blasting the old man off the roof with a fire hose so he would fall down on to the air bag. They decided to let Cassie try to talk to him first and escorted her past the police line into the middle of the front yard.

Mr. Hiemer, who had been shouting at the crowd about making his home safe from aliens, calmed at the sight of Cassie. His wild eyes relaxed and his flared nostrils melted as if he could anchor his mind on her and keep control. She was a beacon of rationality for him to reorient himself by. "Hello Cassie," he said down to her.

"Hello, Mr. Hiemer," Cassie said raising her voice so he could hear yet calmly concealing her stress at boney old Mr. Hiemer precariously perched on the second story gable. "What's up?" she asked nonchalantly.

"Just want to do some work on the house and these people are trying to stop me ..."

"You know you can call me if the house needs work." Cassie's straightforwardness and practicality could bring any situation back to earth. "Mr. Hiemer ... Frosting?"

The old man's eyes sank sheepishly. "It's the only pliant sugar compound I could find to act as a boundary adhesive for the metallic foil. It'll go around the edge of the window to keep their rays from leaking in."

"Mr. Hiemer, come down and talk to me about it. OK ... You and I ... we used to talk. You could get hurt up there. These people care, they want to help." Cassie's sincerity turned her words into a plea.

"Cassie, these people don't care! Some of them aren't even real people!" Mr. Hiemer saw a slender man wearing round glasses with a pointed goatee in the crowd and started shouting again. "The only reason they're trying to stop me is because I know about them! I know ..." He'd been hanging off the side of the gable like King Kong on the Empire State building when suddenly he lost his grip and toppled off the gable. The frail old man's eyes bugged wide as he went sliding down the steeply sloping roof on his stomach before the gasping crowd. There was time for a comical "woop woop woop" yell like one of the Three Stooges as he sailed off the roof with a perfect belly flop on to the airbag making a loud "PLOOF" sound.

Everyone froze for an instant and held their breath at the old man's fate. Slowly, Mr. Hiemer poked his head up from over the airbag. "I'm okay," he said meekly. There was an abbreviated round of polite applause and then the crowd started to break up leaving Cassie standing there in the middle of the yard with her mouth open.


"Now, was that so bad? You had the whole thing wrapped up in five minutes," Tina said as Cassie drove them back home. "You really got that 'make it happen' executive business woman thing down." Tina really admired Cassie and her career but would never want to work as hard as Cassie did.

"Hey, I could have been home an hour ago and we were supposed to go out. If it's not UFOs, it's the county

17

planning committee and then Tanya messed up a pile of appraisal paperwork ..."

"And that's something else," Tina interrupted Cassie's escalating tirade. "You should take it easy on Tanya. She kind of looks up to you and you been riding her really hard lately."

"Well it's my job to be the bitch and there's no one else to do it. I work hard at it and now I'm ready to relax on the couch with a newspaper. Would you hate me forever if I took a rain check on our night out? Tomorrow, I have that property owner's association dinner but we could get together next week." Cassie's voice was tired.

"Well, you deserve to relax! That was great the way you made that old man fall off that roof right into that airbag," Tina said as the car pulled up to her house.

"I didn't 'make' that old man fall off that roof!" Cassie answered as she put the car in park. "What kind of a bitch do you think I am?"

"Of course not. Say Cass, why don't you spend the night at my place tonight? I don't work until tomorrow afternoon. It'll be like a sleep over. We can melt smores in the microwave. It'll be fun and you don't need to be in that apartment all by yourself having nightmares. I know you and you're going sit there doing paperwork till you fall asleep on the couch."

Cassie had to smile at the way Tina really cared. It was something unusual in a life that didn't have time for relationships. "T, I've been alone in that apartment for years and I've done just fine," Cassie said it with the authority of someone making a speech to a hundred people. They both knew she wasn't fine but Cassie was a 'make it happen woman' and she would get her way. "But thanks T. You know you're my best friend."

Cassie watched Tina scamper up to her front door and shouted after her. "I did not 'make' that old man fall off that roof!"

Tina was unique, simple, almost naive with the worldly experience of a bartender that had worked all over the United States. An anxious feeling held Cassie still for a minute as she watched Tina disappear through the front door into her townhouse. She shook the feeling and drove home.

The Mr. Hiemer incident brought closure to Cassie's week. The old man was escorted away by caring professionals who could help him in sort of happy ending. Cassie had come home fully intent on relaxing idly but the pile of paperwork that resided permanently on her kitchen table called to her. It seemed to taunt her, "Come to me, Cassie. I built your life. You need me." It took a forceful act of will to turn her back on the pile and walk into her living room to plop on the couch. In feigned relaxation, she spent some time watching TV but the local news started up with another flying saucer story so she turned it off having heard enough about flying saucers. The sound of the TV faded away and everything began to get quieter and quieter.

She was lying in bed alone with the lights off and a lonely moment settled on her two bedroom apartment. It was Friday and another week had passed. It didn't really mean anything except that she was alone again and she didn't know why it bothered her tonight. She never cared for the social life, her job was socially intensive and she looked forward to the chance to get away from people at the end of the day. She would relax combing through want ads and real estate files looking for her next deal. That's how she had found the property for her pending deal with Supply Management Services, a warehousing and distribution company. Work was her idea of relaxing and whenever she stopped to relax there was just an emptiness that she would fill with plans to make millions of dollars on her next property development.

The feminine floral decor and the shadows cast by the knick knacks on the wall formed complex patterns of light and dark. Lying in bed, she studied the shadows and listened to the silence which seemed to accentuate a sense of loneliness in her life. There weren't even any sounds from the roads or surrounding buildings. She felt completely alone, almost fearful. It was a fear she knew as a child when the night shadows on the wall took on a life of their own forming horrific faces to scowl at her. But now her fear was real, not that there was really anything to be afraid of but the fear itself was real.

Her bedroom seemed so small in the darkness like it was cluttered or crowded. Suddenly she realized that it was crowded, two men stood motionless in the shadows. She wasn't sure at first but without moving she focused her eyes and saw that she was back in her cramp little dorm room where she spent her final two years of college. There were shadowy people standing around that she didn't

22

recognize. This dream didn't even have any of the usual running up and down endless hallways desperately looking for her clothes or late homework. All the people chasing her were already in her room.

Her heart raced and her breathing got shallow as she fought off panic. "I just have to stay still," she thought to herself. "If I don't move they'll go away." But she knew they wouldn't. The bedsprings were rattling quietly from her trembling. "Just pretend to be dead, just don't move ..." One of the men came walking towards her bed and a bright light flashed in her eyes.

Cassie awoke startled by a bright light flooding her room. It was ten o'clock in the morning and her pillow was wet with her tears. She didn't know what happened but fortunately it was Saturday and she wasn't expected in the office. She could remember the fear of a nightmare but she didn't want to recall the details. It was one of the usual anxiety dreams where she was back in school being singled out and harassed by some teacher or group of students. There was one professor in particular from her junior year in college that she always found to be more menacing than most.

Something else she couldn't remember had happened to her in the night. There was some kind of clear jelly smeared between her thighs. She rubbed it and examined it on her fingertips but it evaporated away into nothing. The slime held her spellbound for a long moment before she started fighting with a towel trying to get all traces of it off her skin but there was nothing there. She had imagined it.

She sprang from bed and checked the doors and windows finding them locked and bolted from the inside. Checking the door locks and windows at night was one of her compulsive rituals and she knew there was no chance she left anything unlocked. She would check them each three times every night before bed.

Her first instinct was to call Tina and tell her about it. But Tina's phone rang without answer until Cassie finally hung up and once again she was faced with the tangible silence of her existence. The focal point of her whole life was no more than a pile of papers on the kitchen table. Once the Supply Management Services deal was done then her life would be empty until the next deal put another pile of paperwork in front of her. She ran back to the bedroom and threw herself back into bed to deal with more tears. She knew something would have to change in her life.

Chapter 2

Supply Management Services

Walter Smith wasn't the type of person that cared what other people thought of him but he would never be talking to himself aloud unless he was sure no one else could hear him. Alone in the desert he could rage at his car broken down on the roadside without someone else deciding he was crazy. Without another person to categorize him as a lunatic he could hold on to the idea that he was perfectly sane all the time under all conditions.

"This is unreal!" Walter Smith shouted at the lifeless Buick which especially now seemed to deserve it's ugly gray color and the white splatters of bird droppings on its right front quarter. "The one time the boss is more pissed off than ever. The customer is pissed off, I've got to drive out here on my day off and have you crap out on me in the middle of nowhere." People broke down in the middle of nowhere all the time but for him on this drive at this time it was the culmination of personal insult. It isolated him psychologically as did the empty desert around him.

Less than a year ago, Walter Smith was an environmental research scientist with a career and now he was delivering toilet paper for his uncle's business, Supply Management Services. His concerns about his boss and his job gave way to concerns over food and water when he realized that he hadn't seen another vehicle for an hour. He certainly wasn't dressed for desert survival in his ill fitting grey slacks and a cyanotic blue short sleeve dress shirt with a pocket weighed down by pens, pencils, little screwdrivers and even a little penlight. His shiny black shoes looked good but were really made out of cheap vinyl that hurt his feet. The idea that he arrived at the leading edge technology research center not as a scientist but as a guy bringing toilet paper made the situation that much more devastating.

Walter knew that this road was a major traffic artery to a huge construction site of a research facility called the 'Massive Superconducting Super Collider' or 'MSSC'. In the remote desert of West Texas it was an epicenter for the ebb and flow of hundreds of construction workers. He was certain that someone would come along soon but in case they didn't, he started to assess the inventory of the car. There was a half liter jug of spring water, a bag of chips and a pack of gum.

In the back seat, there were three cases of toilet paper and four more cases in the trunk. The large boxes of toilet paper had been left off of a shipment from Supply Management Services and the construction company that had ordered it needed it in a bad way. They bitched out his boss who then bitched him out. It fell to Walter as warehouse manager to fix everything by driving the toilet paper personally out to the site. Toilet paper could easily become something critical given the size of the job involving hundreds of workers and the remoteness of the site.

Hours seemed to go by as Walter waited on the roadside but he never felt alone because everywhere he went he carried a contingent of imaginary characters in his head. He wrote science fiction stories in his spare time outside of work and always had a plot playing out in his mind. His latest was a love story about a couple on a planet where gravity was slowly reversing and over the centuries their society had to adapt to hanging on instead of standing up. The story ends sadly as one of the star crossed lovers loses her grip and falls up into the sky to perish in the planet's thin stratosphere. Walter's stories would take on lives of their own giving him a whole different reality to flee his mundane world which was isolated by emptiness on all sides. He could escape to a world of bizarre aliens, exotic planets and alternate dimensions inhabited by strange intelligences.

Walter had written another story that could always absorb him into the world of his imagination. This story featured a character like himself who joined a record of the month club back when musical recordings came on vinyl disks. The record club offered 6 records to new members. The protagonist then collected all the free sample records plus a dozen more on the no money thirty day guarantee without paying. By the time the record club demanded their money, he had already moved to a new address and started collecting more free records under a new name. The amount of money was trivial at the time but it continued to accrue interest and penalties for many centuries after the man's death. It grew to a debt of hundreds of billions of dollars financially crippling the record club which was now an international multi-media recording company with subsidiaries in many industries. Finally, the record company in the year two thousand seven hundred and fifty three sends a killer robot back in time to kill the man before he joins the club. There's a fierce battle and the hero conquers by pushing the robot into the chute of a giant meat grinder in an abandoned dog food factory. Some of Walter's friends did tell him that the story sounded familiar and had probably been done before.

Walter's digital watch had gone blank so he couldn't tell how long he'd been there. The shadows showed the sun moving to the east but that was a mirage like the shimmering water he saw spreading in wavy lines rising

31

through the warm air. He could see a metallic structure miles down the road reflecting the sun. It looked round like a silver coliseum building but was still too far away to see any detail. He knew the construction site was less than five miles away and was under a two hour walk. That structure was probably the center and there had to be somebody there with the authority to accept the toilet paper delivery. The desert sun was out in a clear sky but the fall temperature kept it a relatively cool eighty degrees. He resolutely decided he would start walking.

It would be easy enough to carry one case of toilet paper. That should hold them until he could get a ride back out to the car to get the other six cases. Suddenly in his mind he could see the absurd image of him carrying this large box of toilet paper, twelve rolls high and ten wide and ten deep, through the desert. His image was rescued by an imaginary beautiful woman in a small two seater sports car who pulled up to give him a ride. She saw that she had no room in her car for his large box so she sped off leaving him standing there. His elderly mother's harsh voice antagonized him from the grave as it often did, "You'll never find a girl." Startled, he realized that he had drifted off into one of his daydreams again. Daydreaming was the life long habit which some people blamed for a lot of his problems in life but he always thought of it as a gift.

Walter decided that the toilet paper would stay with the car however the idea of showing up in front of hundreds of construction workers without any toilet paper didn't seem right either. He put three rolls of the toilet paper into a canvas gym bag he found wadded up in the corner of his trunk. He looked at the meager three rolls in the bag and added five more rolls, paused then obsessively packed six more on top of that. He also packed the bag of chips, the water and all the paperwork to deal with the incident. There was a portable tape player with headphones and a cassette of Kurt Vonnegut being interviewed about UFOs but the battery was dead so he tossed it back into the glove compartment. He locked up the car and strode off down the road ready for anything.

His steps were lifted by the vision of himself bursting into the project manager's office with a roll of toilet paper just in the nick of time. It would be just like his favorite sci-fi action hero Major Matt Mason (Walter was probably the only thirty-eight year old that watched the animated Saturday morning cartoon). It would be the real tangible job satisfaction of accomplishing something physically instead of in a theory or hypothesis. "Yes, that's the spirit that made Supply Management Services the best in the industry," he thought to himself with smug confidence. The boss would be happy and mention it to his uncle. He caught a glimpse of something out of the corner of his eye flashing silently through the sky but he missed it. The desert air created all kinds of optical illusions.

His vehicle faded behind him into the desert and Walter could see something ahead on the road. He was soon close enough to discern four army trucks parked on the side of the road like troops had been delivered there. This wasn't too unusual for this kind of high tech civilian project. The army itself wasn't interested in a particle accelerator; they probably just provided the security so bad guys wouldn't get the technology. The military could certainly give him a ride.

The canvas covered flatbed trucks were all empty. Walter explored them inside and out finding that one truck had a two way radio but it didn't work. Everything about the trucks seemed fine and they even had the keys and gas in them but turning the key produced no results not even a clicking or a light on the dashboard. He looked back up and down the road. The main office of the site couldn't be more than a couple of miles further. He was trying to focus on the round metallic structure in the distance when something on the ground caught his attention.  It was a footprint.

Walter looked at the ground and saw footprints from heavy army boots everywhere.  Dozens of troops coming out of the back of the trucks left a distinct trail.  The tracks milled and gathered around the trucks then marched off into the desert where he followed them a short distance from the road to a clearing where they stopped.  There were no return tracks and no place to go.  He pondered the truck conundrum for a moment.  "This was probably some military training exercise," he thought.  The army could be doing some air pick up training as they sometimes do in the desert.  He reasoned that helicopters probably picked these guys up but that image had helicopter rotors blowing away the footprints in the sand.  The answer was obvious to Walter after another moment of study.  They must have used dirigibles to pick up the troops for a training mission.  Dirigibles were silent and could land or take off anywhere without a trace. One of the armed forces was obviously practicing anti-terrorist dirigible tactics. It was a comfort to know that the government was ready for anything. He continued on his way down the road.

Walter Smith had never seen a particle accelerator in his short career as a scientist. He knew that when construction was finished, this facility would be one of the largest in the world and the only way he would ever get close to it was delivering toilet paper. Walter was a washed-up biologist and only a small group of elite physicists would get to direct the research that went on here. Millions of dollars were being spent on a circular race track ten miles across where the aristocracy of science could accelerate electrons to the speed of light. They would ultimately unravel the weave of reality while important issues like clean air and water got little attention.

Like Walter, the rest of the world didn't see the point in tinkering with immutable things like gravity and neutrons.

Most people didn't even know what a supercollider was and they certainly weren't willing to spend a hundred million dollars on one. As funding got scarcer, the project teetered on the brink of non-existence threatening to disappear from the desert and the mind of the world completely.

Walter's romance for any science had been lost after a few years of commercial environmental science. He got a job right out of college at a private lab that the government had contracted to genetically engineer less intelligent fish which would be easier for sportsmen to catch. Next he ended up on a project researching methane outputs of beef cattle and its impact on the atmosphere as a greenhouse gas. He spent months monitoring a small herd of cattle wearing diapers. Each diapered cow had a corrugated hose coming out of its butt to carry gases to a pack strapped on its back where measurements were made. The ridiculous site of diapered cattle and the gory job of changing the

38

diapers sent Walter fleeing industrial science only to end up delivering toilet paper for his uncle. He had to keep telling himself that all of it was only temporary until he became a famous science fiction writer.

From the air, it was a perfectly round trench in a flat featureless desert like an immense crop circle and would have been a perfect secret UFO landing site. It was no wonder that when people saw this gigantic, high security, high tech thing out in the desert they came to the conclusion that UFOs and the government were involved. Even decades after science eradicated the idea of little green men from Mars, some people still believed in them and gave them an intangible life. Once the facility was a reality, the mark in the desert would fade and the only trace would be some power lines, transformers and a small entrance with a driveway leading underground.

Walter had never bought into any of that government cover-up-of-extraterrestrials-at-Roswell-conspiracy. His family fit the suburban stereotype growing up so he believed that the government was always acting in the best interest of the people and sometimes they had to keep secrets for national security. He had already established that all the abandoned army vehicles here were part of a covert training exercise involving antiterrorist dirigibles but then he came upon some bicycles left on the side of the road. They were the rugged ten speed mountain bikes painted army green with 'Property of US Government' stenciled in black on each. It was probably some program allowing impoverished inner city kids to hike and bike in the desert. Walter could have used a bike but they'd probably be back any minute and he knew better than to tamper with government property.

Walter Smith was on a mission that transcended government and even the questions that the MSSC asked about the quantum physical stardust in our molecules. He carried fourteen rolls of life's most fundamental truth, toilet paper. It was destined to be used in the final result of the life process and was a vital link in the existence of the supercollider. Hundreds of people just over a mile ahead in the desert were in desperate need of that truth. With a new story brewing in his head, he continued his journey with renewed vigor past more abandoned vehicles and came walking up to the front gate of the construction complex.

There was no activity, the gates were closed and the guard house was empty like a holiday or something. Everything was completely still and silent without even the scurrying of desert creatures on the sand. Even circling buzzards would have been some comfort. A few miles further ahead a round metallic structure several stories high and hundreds of feet across sat at the center of the ninety-two thousand acre site. If he could get through the gate someone would have to be there. When the boss hears how much work it took to deliver this he'd be so proud of Walter that it could mean a serious pay raise.

41

A dark figure was taking shape on the horizon in the shimmering air. It wasn't traveling down the road but across the open desert coming right at him. It was a man on a horse plodding slowly along. At first, the man and horse looked very tiny like a toy only a few yards away. Walter knew this to be an illusion caused by the featureless desert expanse. Squinting and rubbing his eyes, he then saw the man walking beside the horse. Neither Walter, the man, nor the horse noticed the formation of slivery lights flash silently overhead like reflections of the desert sun cast from an opening car door. The formation moved too quickly and erratically to be anything more than light.

Walter was contemplating the slow moving man and horse when suddenly his boss appeared in front of him shouting, "Where have you been all day!" The vision tore Walter's attention from the old man on the horizon and prompted him to start searching the entrance to the site. The guard house was a small air conditioned booth. The sliding glass door was open allowing him to see the gate controls and an official looking phone. It was the kind of phone that had no way to dial and it was red so it obviously was connected to somebody important. He decided that he wouldn't disturb the phone unless it became absolutely necessary.

There was a video camera mounted up on the guard house watching the gate. Walter decided he would try to communicate with it and positioned himself in front of the camera. "Hello. Hello," he said bashfully. The camera didn't have any lights on it or anything to indicate that anyone was watching. "I'm Walter Smith. Mr. Bloedell of Supply Management Services sent me." He wanted them to know that he was here on serious business so he produced a roll from his bag and held it up for the camera to see. "I have toilet paper ..." There was no response from the camera so he decided it wasn't a real camera but one of those cheap mock-ups that are supposed to scare away prowlers.  He froze suddenly and became aware of two small children standing behind him watching.  When he whipped around the old man and his horse were standing there.

The old man had to have a helicopter or something because there was no way he could have covered that half mile so quickly.  His tattered dirty old clothes and skin said that he didn't own a helicopter but a look in his eyes said that he had something.  The horse was old and tattered also but was calm and relaxed like he'd only walked a few steps.  The old unshaven face gave a gap tooth grin then said simply and enigmatically, "Howdy."

Walter stood for a moment staring slack jaw at the old man who looked exactly like an old man wandering in the desert would look like.  He shook the spell and stammered, "uh hello ... uh I was looking for someone in charge but there's no one here."  He didn't really believe that the old man knew anything but he had to ask.

44

"Yep ... nobody here," the old man affirmed. There was something sinister in the way he said it and in the way he cast an eye to the vacant guard house. "... and you ain't in charge?" A weathered old eyebrow rose.

"Well ... No I'm not in charge but I'm sure the site manager will meet me personally when he hears I've arrived," Walter said confidently as he patted the bag he carried.

"I guess right now I'm in charge," the old man said giving Walter Smith a level look then walking off toward the gate leaving his horse. Walter panicked as he saw the old man reach out to touch the electrified gate that crossed the road. Instead of getting knocked down by a bolt of electricity, the old man pulled on the gate and it slid back into the fence. It moved easily like it was on rollers and it took no effort from the old man to open it completely. "You may go in now," he said obligingly.

"Wait," Walter called out after the old man as he started trespassing onto the site. "Someone should report that this station is unmanned. It could be some kind of problem." He was not only concerned for the security of this high tech area but for his own mission.

"Well come on," the old man beckoned. "You can report." He then turned stepping deliberately across the fence threshold and began to walk off down the dirt road which pierced the horizon with a straight line to the center of the site. The twelve foot high chain link fence had no corners and formed another concentric circle outside the collider site. From the ground, it created the illusion that the fence went on forever in both directions.

Walter Smith went in and caught up to walk beside the old man. "What about your horse?" he asked.

"Oh he'll be along." The old man's eyes fixed on the metal structure in the distance as he walked.

## Chapter 3

### You may go in now

Cassie was reading a magazine in the reception area of Dr. Carter's office when a small wooden figure of a horse sitting on a shelf caught her attention. Dr. Carter's reception area, unlike so many bright sterile medical waiting areas, was accented in dark hardwoods and decorated like an old library but it was still a place where people brought pain to be treated. The family magazine that she was reading couldn't hold her attention with its tepid articles and recipes so her mind had drifted around the room and had been captured by the random knick-knack. "You may go in now," the receptionist said startling Cassie back into the world of the reception area.

Cassie hesitated before she touched the sliding hardwood doors as if she feared an electric shock. She knew that once she went in she was admitting that her problem was real. Once that threshold was crossed and that admission was made, there would be no returning. There would be no way to make it unreal because even if she could erase it you couldn't erase the mark left by erasing it. It would be free in the world to take on a life of its own with its own agenda. The best she could hope for was to bring it under control and learn to live with it.

Cassie slid open the door and even after all the years away, slipping into the office was as familiar and comforting as it had ever been. She realized only now how empty her life had been of any intimacy. It was strange how she didn't miss it.

"Cassie, it's good to see you. I was surprised to see your name in my appointment book after all these years." Dr. Sylvia Carter was a lot like Cassie in that she was also a successful self made business woman. Being fifteen years older than Cassie, she had the salt and pepper hair making her mature in their relationship but not enough to make it a parent-child relationship. "You look like you're well," the Doctor said at the sight of Cassie dressed like the CEO of a huge corporation.

"I am doing well," Cassie said sitting down on the fine leather couch which was right at home in Dr. Carter's lavish hardwood office. "I own nine rental properties now and I'm thinking about buying another."

"That's so good to hear. You must be putting in a lot of hours." Dr. Carter was beaming a proud smile as she sat in a matching overstuffed leather chair that sat compassionately next to the couch. "In my business, I don't always get to see any results. You could show a lot of women survivors a real success story." The Doctor had a slow measured way of speaking even in social situations. It matched the gentle way she held her hands folded in her lap.

"After the attack, I thought I'd never leave the house again. It was the first thing I felt in the morning and it followed me every moment of the day." Even years later, Cassie still shuddered actively working to forget the violent assault that shattered her life. "The feeling was constantly in me like I was going to start throwing up but you really helped me through it. I don't know how I could've dealt with it without your help. Things have changed a lot for me since then."

"You say you've dealt with it," the Doctor interrupted. "But now you're back. Are you okay?"

50

"My medical Doctor said I should talk to you," Cassie explained. "I've been having these spells where I have trouble breathing and my heart beat goes crazy. They ran all kinds of tests on me and couldn't find anything so they said I should consult a 'mental health specialist'." She looked up sheepishly at the Doctor and the business woman power trip disappeared leaving a six year old girl. "They think that I'm going crazy but they didn't want to tell me."

"Have you been having any other problems?" the Doctor asked as if she knew there was more.

"Well ... I don't know." Cassie had to wrestle the idea from her mind. She felt her throat closing up at the thought of talking about it. "I'm having nightmares." She forced out the words wanting to believe that some 'thing' was wrong which could be removed surgically or treated with antibiotics. It was difficult to accept that the problem could be her.

"Nightmares?" the Doctor said in her therapeutic way that asked Cassie to 'tell me more'.

"Yes, almost every night, at least two or three times a week. It's just all kinds of nightmares. Sometimes I'm back in college walking the halls looking for my class, sometimes I'm just paralyzed and can barely breathe. Once I dreamt that my teeth were broken and I was crunching them around in my mouth like broken glass." Cassie faltered before talking about the nightmare that dominated them. "The worst of them all ... I'm examined."

"Examined?" the Doctor asked with a raised eyebrow. Cassie had just revealed it wasn't a normal nightmare.

"Yes, it's like some kind of medical exam. But they're not really looking for anything they're just finding ways to hurt me." Cassie's voice broke slightly as she looked down at her hands. She fidgeted nervously realizing that every waking hour she had a phone, a folder or something in her hands. Now, for the first time in years her hands were empty and she felt naked. "They want to hurt me in front of other people, like I'm on display."

"Hurt you?" The Doctor had slipped right into her role by drawing more information from the patient by turning her last words into a question. Cassie knew the game but she wanted answers also so she played along like word association. The dark hardwoods and subdued lighting of the quiet office made it easy for Cassie to focus on her dreams.

"They have needles and tools that they use on me," Cassie said slowly letting herself remember more. She would have never allowed any of it into her mind if she wasn't in the comfort and safety of the Doctor's office. "But it's more ... They want to humiliate me."

"Who's doing this to you?" the Doctor asked leaning over closer to Cassie comforting her with a face of concern and wisdom.

"I don't know ...  People ...  I can't ever remember their faces.  I can't move."  Cassie pursued the vague horrible images through the gaps in her memory.  She wanted to remember but was driven back by something that scared her.  "I remember bright lights; they take me away under these bright lights.  There's a metal table like an operating table."  Cassie paused to draw a deep breath and didn't want to remember anymore.  "I wake up crying every time."  Something deep inside her made the conscious decision to close the door and stop remembering.

The Doctor could sense the fear in her voice.  She knew that if it was bad enough for Cassie to make it an issue it had to be really bad.  "Do you think the dreams have anything to do with what happened five years ago?" the Doctor asked directly yet somehow spared the pain in the question.

"I don't know ... It's the only thing I can think of that left me with the feeling of fear and violation that I have in these dreams." Cassie drew a breath as she gently reached out to the memory. She had felt like she had so completely conquered the experience long ago. At the time all she knew was that she was walking from her office to the deli at lunch when someone struck her head from behind with a heavy object. She woke up beaten so severely that she had been in a coma for two weeks. The Doctors and police told her that she had been the victim of a serial rapist and out of three others she was the only one to survive. The man was captured by the police attacking another woman and killed an officer trying to escape. He was cornered in an alleyway and after a gunfight died in a torrent of police gunfire leaving his body an unrecognizable pulp. She remembered the gruesome police pictures of the body and could watch his death in slow motion whenever she chose. On the advice of the Doctors she went to some support group meetings but their shared stories only served to fill the void in her memory with horrific visions. Seeing her attacker's

55

body like two hundred pounds of hamburger planted in the ground ended his existence in her world forever without return. There were some other demons coming after her.

"How's you're work going? Have you had a lot of job stress?" the Doctor asked changing the subject allowing Cassie some distance from the pain.

"I'm working harder than ever but I love it. The whole business is my baby that I built myself and it's very rewarding. I don't think it would give me bad dreams ... and why now after all these years?" Working was Cassie's escape from everything and she looked back on the last five years like one long day at the office.

"Stress is subtle; it could be sneaking up on you," the Doctor speculated. "What are your relationships like?" the Doctor asked tipping Cassie off to another strategic change of subject. "Do you go out with your friends?"

"Well sometimes I go out with my friend Tina. We'll go out to have sushi, sometimes we'll rent a movie and stay in." Cassie had to struggle to come up with an answer that didn't make her sound like a shut-in. It was an uncomfortable struggle against a realization that she had some fundamental problem.

"What about men?" the Doctor pursued. "Do you date?"

Cassie rolled her eyes at the Doctor. "I don't even have time for a house plant. Actually, a house plant doesn't dig in the refrigerator and is a lot more interesting than most of the men I meet anyway." In her mind, she composed her perfect dream guy for a split second. He would be a broad shouldered man in military uniform like her father was. But the fact that she went out of her way to keep intimate relationships out of her life said something about herself she didn't want to know. The entire meeting with the Doctor had turned a magnifying spotlight on her that she couldn't and wouldn't face.

"Cassie," the Doctor said leaning forward. "What do you think the dreams mean?" The Doctor's compassionate gaze was telling Cassie that she knew the answer.

"Look Doctor…" Cassie said resolutely. "I'm sorry that I wasted your time. But I think I'll be okay. I'm sure I'm just going through some phase… maybe a midlife crisis."

"Tell me. Is there anything specific that sets off these spells he talked about? Is there something that makes you particularly nervous?" The Doctor asked talking past Cassie's attempt to end the session.

Cassie had to stop and really think but couldn't put her finger on a specific fear just general fear. "Snakes, I guess," she finally answered.

"Ha," the Doctor laughed. "We all have that fear. What are you nervous about right now? Where do you feel safe?"

Cassie had to think again but it seemed that she used to feel safe at home in her apartment. The idea of traveling and strange surroundings definitely made her uncomfortable. "New people and new surroundings put me on edge ... I feel most comfortable at home ... my apartment."

"Cassie, you may be developing a slight touch of agoraphobia. When was the last time you took some time off for a vacation?"

The question caught Cassie off guard and she had to stop with no real answer.

"If you can't remember, then it's been too long. You know, I could give you something that would help you sleep better but that's really not what's going on here," the Doctor said with a gently diagnostic look that made Cassie feel like she was being accused of something. "Remember, I know you."

Cassie knew she couldn't hide anything from the Doctor, even the things she wanted to hide from herself. In only a few minutes the Doctor zeroed in on her workaholic lifestyle as a source of dysfunction instead of the source of stability and comfort that Cassie saw. Like a sudden bright light shining in her face, it made Cassie uncomfortable. "But Dr… there is nothing in my dreams about work." She didn't want to believe that her career which sheltered her from the world was hurting her. "Work is where I feel the most empowered. These dreams are more like being back in school, social anxiety, test anxiety. You know like sitting in class naked without your homework."

"Dreams aren't about things they're about feelings. What are the feelings in your dreams?" the Doctor asked.

"Fear, helplessness ... Violation …" All the words that her dreams conjured up kept taking her back to the violent assault that first brought her to Dr. Carter five years ago. The lights in the office flickered for a moment drawing their attention interrupting them but then returning to normal. "I hope we're not about to have another black out," Cassie remarked.

"The one of the good things about being a psychiatrist is that I can work by candlelight if I have to," the Doctor quipped before refocusing her attention. "Cassie, dreams aren't run by cause and effect. Actually it's like life; everything is completely related but only in a general way. Sometimes the things with the most obvious impact on our lives are only coincidence and the real impacts are made by people and things outside of our lives that we aren't even aware of. Then there are unbelievable coincidences that are just coincidence. Sometimes," the Doctor continued. "We get so caught up in our jobs that we forget that we have thinking, feeling people inside us. I'll bet you drive a really expensive car."

"Well, a Jaguar actually ... but I got a really good deal on it."

"Okay, Cassie, I'm getting the picture of someone working lots of hours, dealing with tens of thousands of dollars ..."

"Hundreds of thousands," Cassie corrected.

"Okay, in any case, big money, big stress, big business woman image. Cassie, don't you see it? It's a lot to keep up. Years go by with your shoulders hunched, your jaw clenched, the next thing you know you have four digit blood pressure. Cassie, my real prescription to you is to slow down and relax." Then she asked, "What do you really want in life? More property? More money? What you want, just like everybody else, is to know what it is you want."

"Look Doctor, I just remembered I have to go." Cassie got up from the couch digging in her purse for her car keys avoiding eye contact with the Doctor. "I'm sorry. I'm sure I'll be fine. Thank you."

"Okay, Okay." The Doctor knew she had moved too quickly. "Just promise that you'll call me if it doesn't get better. Okay?"

Cassie was still thinking about what the Doctor said as she left the building where the Doctor's office was. They had only spent an hour together but she knew she would carry the session inside her for days. Love, intimacy and someone to share her life with, were the same things everyone wanted. Why now when Cassie had so much was it all so important to her and how could she feel so lonely? She'd agreed to return next week if things hadn't gotten better. Somehow, Cassie knew that this was all more complicated than a couple of pills and some time off. There was an emptiness in the past few years that was painful to look at.

Cassie found a traffic jam on the busy street in front of the mirror and metal building. Pedestrians were stopped on the sidewalk and cars were stopped with their drivers standing outside them. Everyone was looking up at the slice of sky visible between the high rise buildings. Cars were honking and there was a panicked chatter among the people. She walked out onto the sidewalk looking up like everybody else. "What's going on?" she asked a man on the sidewalk.

Cassie wouldn't have normally talked to a complete stranger but the intense commotion warranted it. She suddenly realized when the man turned around that he was a clown. His frizzy gold afro wig was close enough to blonde to take away from his painted face and red rubber nose for a moment. She had to step back for his clowniness to sink in.

"This thing out of the sky came down between the buildings!" the clown reported excitedly as he advanced on her. "It was huge." The clown wore a big plywood sign that read, 'Pizza Buffet $3.99' with an arrow that Cassie assumed pointed to a pizza parlor when the clown stood in the right spot.

"A thing?" Cassie asked retreating from his advance chastising herself silently for inadvertently picking the only clown in the crowd.

"It started like a big ball of light. It somehow folded in and flattened out like a plate so it could fit down between the buildings."

A plate ... like a saucer?" Cassie asked skeptically. "A 'flying' saucer?" She had to raise her voice over the noises in the street.

"Oh bullshit!" another stranger interrupted. "It was some kind of big balloon like they fly at parades. It probably just broke lose. I'm sure they'll catch it at the Fordson Street Bridge." This non-clown stranger seemed to be very sure of himself.

"Parade balloons don't have lights on them. This thing had lights on it," the clown protested. "This thing's got lights all over it." Cassie had already started off down the street. Whatever it was, it was over and if anything real had happened she would get a better account from the six o'clock news than from either of these clowns.

She stopped at the bar where Tina worked on the way home. Tina hadn't been in to work and they were as concerned as Cassie was. The fact that Cassie showed up asking if they had seen Tina alarmed the people who worked there even more. Everyone agreed that if someone didn't hear from her in another day they would call the police. There was a chance that she had met a guy who took her away for the weekend but Cassie would have been the first to know if that had happened. Tina was the only person that Cassie had ever shared that type of relationship with. On the way home, a shooting star had stopped in the sky to warn her of something astrological before it continued its streak.

Cassie's apartment always had a calming effect on her. It was half of a duplex with a quiet, confirmed, old bachelor renting the other half. Lately, her panic attacks had gotten so bad that she was living her life around them, rushing home when the anxiety got too much for her to handle. As she closed the door behind her, she latched the little chain, turned the deadbolt and locked the knob. Three locks that she would check every night three times before bed. She stood in the hallway and tried to relax, counting her pulse which was seventy four beats per minute. It was high for her but the beats were strong and regular. Even after three thousand dollars worth of cardiac tests she still worried that the regular beat would suddenly stop and she was constantly coming up with scenarios to survive long enough to call help.

That night lying in bed, she watched the local news and saw nothing about any U.F.O. downtown but as she flipped through the channels, an image on the national news caught her eye. It was an aerial view of an immense circle carved in the desert. She listened to the newscaster and it turned out that it didn't have anything to do with U.F.O.s but it was some new research facility under construction in west Texas. It was called the Super Collider. She turned off the TV then reached over to turn off the lamp but hesitated. She could feel someone watching her and the feeling demanded some action from her. Her rational mind would not allow her to check the closet for stranger waiting or worse yet to look under the bed for monsters. There couldn't be anyone in her bedroom but the battle going on in her consciousness had created a foe as fleshy as an ax murderer hiding at the foot of her bed.

Cassie knew it would be a bad night, she just knew it. It may have been all usual crap on the local news or the fact that she had hundreds of thousands of investment dollars teetering for existence in zoning committees. Somehow by seeing the Doctor, she was admitting that the problem was real and the more she thought about it, the more it fed on her attention and grew. Everything around her seemed to carry a sense of foreboding that she could not shake. None of these feelings were real but they persisted as tangibly as a dense fog. She thought at first it was another anxiety attack and for a moment there was a comforting familiarity in it but that comfort couldn't be tolerated.

Cassie snapped off the lamp and in the same quick movement pulled the sheets over her head. She knew there couldn't be anyone in her bedroom and under the covers she felt like she could hide from the idea of people in her bedroom. She snuggled deeper under the covers pulling them tighter around herself but felt then pulling back like they were hung on something. Then she realized the covers were pulling back. Panic quickened her breathing to panting as she struggled in a tug of war with someone at the foot of her bed. She knew she was alone but couldn't deny the feeling that someone was trying to pull the covers off of her. As long as the bed sheets covered her head she could believe that she was just having a dream but the steady persistent tugging kept trying to uncover her. She cursed herself for not looking under the bed and checking the closet. The fact was that someone could be in her bedroom and with that realization the covers were violently whipped off the bed and she saw shadowy figures standing around her in the darkness.

She screamed and bolted upright in her bed but nothing happened, no sound, no movement. She was paralyzed. It was like a lucid dream where she knew she was dreaming because the situation couldn't be real. Yet, she couldn't wake herself. Like so many nightmares she had before, she laid paralyzed in her panties and T-shirt as people gathered around her. One of them grabbed her arm and she knew it was real. She couldn't turn her head to look directly at any of the people around her but could sense them in her peripheral vision. A fleshy hand maintained its grip on her like a snake coiled around her arm. The shadows surrounding her were inhumanely short like evil gnomes.

All she could do was cry, sobbing through her mouth falling open under its own weight. There were no questions in her mind of why they were here or what they wanted, just begging and pleading that they would leave. She didn't care if it was real or a dream, she just wanted it to stop.

More of the powerful, fleshy hands took hold of her pulling her off the bed. Her body fell on the floor with a thud that still couldn't wake her up. As they jostled around she caught glimpse of one of the hands holding her and that stopped her breathing. It was cadaver gray with only three long fingers. Her mind struggled with the image trying to see it as a fake rubber hand, part of a Halloween costume with a "Made in China" label. But it was real flesh, it was alive. As she lay on the floor, they gathered close and someone cradled her head from behind so she could see the face of one of her captors in the moon light.

A small man knelt over her bringing his face closer to hers. Before she could even make out the details of the face she could sense its rage. By talking to the Doctor, she would try to deny them existence and now they would show her a face that she couldn't deny. The first thing she saw was the big black slanted eyes. They weren't the shiny black eyes of a squirrel but the fluid filled eyes of an insect set in a man's face. But it wasn't a normal man; he had dead gray skin with no wrinkles. His face had to have been disfigured because he had no nose just nostrils. The entire face was alive and twitching. The slit of a mouth had no lips but it flexed and opened wide like it had the muscular lips of a horse. The face contorted horribly and hissed wetly at her. Her terror broke through and she started to scream bringing her into sharp focus in front of the strangers so they could get a firm grip on her body. They were beyond anything sexual, they wanted her vulnerable. Her screaming and writhing didn't seem to affect them; it was the type of energy discharge they wanted. Two of them took her by the ankles and dragged her away like she was weightless, like a balloon on the string pulled by a child.

Every split second brought new horrors. She was no longer in her apartment but in a large round room with a table as a platform in the middle. In a foggy blur of gray three fingered hands she was put on the table then turned face down. Some invisible force at her wrists and ankles pulled her spread eagle. Straining her head around, she could see little gray men scurrying around her preparing for some procedure. She struggled some but a blue spotlight hit her in the back causing a pain in her chest which made it hard to breathe much less struggle.

They held stainless steel instruments with blades, prongs and needles. Just their shapes suggested forcing tissues open, puncturing skin and cutting samples from internal organs. She could almost understand what they were saying but the voices were distant and dreamlike as if she was hearing their thoughts. Their contempt of her and everything about her filled the air. They needed her but didn't even give her the regard of a filthy beast of burden or an animal to be eaten. It was more like a bacteria in a lab being used to generate pharmaceutical hormones, some of them thought she wasn't even real, just their own consciousness reflecting in the reality barrier. Back in the shadows she got a glimpse of a tall bearded man watching over like he was in charge but he stepped back and disappeared into the dark.

Cassie could just sob as the blue light crushed her down on the table and her hands and ankles were being pulled in different directions. Deep inside, she still couldn't accept what was happening to her and even if this was all real she wouldn't allow herself into the horror of the moment. She felt someone pull her panties down enough to expose her butt and she was flooded with old anxieties. Somehow she knew the only reason they left them on her at all was to humiliate her more and make it all more real and personal. They allowed her to see one of them pouring a slimy clear lubricant over some metal pronged instrument that seemed to flex open and closed like a three finger hand. This wasn't a bad dream or a hallucination, these people were hurting her and nothing could stop them.

Her breathing was down to quick shallow panting as she sensed they were about to do something to her. The shallow panting started catching up to her then deteriorated into hyperventilation and she passed out. Panic broke out around her as her body went limp. They shook her roughly trying to revive her while alarms started beeping and lights flickered. At the moment she blacked out, a little dark haired girl around five years old toddled into the room wearing a light blue dress. The black eyes that had been so intensely focused on Cassie whipped around to the child who was staring at the scene in total innocence. The little girl gazed in magic wonder at the spindly little grey people like they were elves or fairies but knew she wasn't allowed to play with them. "Bye, bye," she said with a sad smile.

Cassie woke up alone in the middle of the night momentarily relieved to be alone but then the depths of her loneliness seized her. She was more than alone in bed she was alone in the world especially since her mother died. It still hurt her after all these years. Tanya, her only employee, would disappear every day after five o'clock to a world Cassie knew nothing about. Everyone else in her life was either a buyer or seller. Tina had been gone almost a week. Slowly, vague, horrific memories of the night crept into her emptiness making her nauseous. But she still wasn't sure what if anything had happened.

The apartment was still and dark as she slipped out of bed and pulled on a bathrobe to look around. Everything in her bedroom seemed in order and undisturbed but just outside the doorway she walked into the silhouette of a man standing in her living room. The man stood perfectly still in the split second that he and Cassie locked eyes while she tried to decide that he was real. As the details of an old man's face assembled itself in the dark room she suddenly realized that there really was a man in her apartment.

Cassie started screaming and staggering backwards searching the shadowy wall for a light switch knocking down hanging pictures. Each scream sent the stranger reeling backward falling on to the couch where he struggled to regain his balance and get back on his feet. Cassie's searching hand fell on yesterday's half read newspaper on the table which she flung at the man sending a blizzard of paper about the room further confounding the stranger. "Get Away! Get Away!" she screamed with all her breath, stumbling her way to a light switch on the other side of the room. The light came on and froze the scene of

Tilden Abernathy cowering on Cassie's couch with pages of the newspaper fluttering down around him. "Tilden! What the hell are you doing here?" Cassie screeched knocking him back onto the couch with her voice.

Tilden Abernathy was the sixty year old retired bachelor who rented the other half of the duplex where Cassie lived. Their separate townhouses shared a common entrance hall but there was no reason for him to be in her living room. Only then did she realize that he was actually cowering in the fetal position on her couch saying, "I'm sorry, I'm sorry ... It's Brutus ..." He was actually trying to shield himself with a sheet of newspaper. "Brutus … Brutus."

"What!? What!" Cassie screeched at the traumatized man. Suddenly, she felt sorry for how pathetic he looked then she felt bad.

"My cat, Brutus, has been missing all day!" Tilden said taking advantage of the break in Cassie's tempest to try to explain. "I was looking out front to see if he had come

78

home and your front door was wide open." He could see she was starting to relax so he stopped talking to catch his breath.

"My front door ... was wide open?" Cassie felt more foolish for the way she had been screaming at the sweet old guy. "My door was open and you walked into my place?" She didn't specifically remember locking the front door that night but she checks three locks three times every night before bed compulsively. There's no way she would leave it completely open. "Completely open?"

"I walked up and I could hear you crying inside like you needed help." He was finally starting to reassemble himself and tightening and primping his soft blue terry cloth night robe. "Are you okay?"

Cassie really didn't know. How could she scream at this man who lived next door and how could she leave her front door open? Did she leave her front door open? She plopped down on the couch next to Tilden who recoiled from her still traumatized. All the screaming had drained her. Suddenly she realized that Tilden was still staring at her waiting for an answer. "Oh yes, I'm okay. I'm so sorry for screaming but you scared me. I was having a nightmare. I mean ..." she hesitated. "You didn't see anyone here did you?"

"No, I didn't see anyone. Who was here?"

"No nobody, I was just having a bad dream ... thanks for checking on me. I'm really sorry I screamed at you." Cassie gave him a weak smile.

"Oh that's okay; I guess we really scared each other." Tilden got up off the couch and bundled himself to leave. "You'll let me know if you see Brutus around." There was something lonely about the way he said it and shuffled away still recovering from their meeting. Cassie wished she could help him. She could relate to his loneliness and wondered if he was a vision of her own future. She decided she would call Dr. Carter and the decision made her feel better until she realized the only person she had to talk to was someone who was paid to listen. After locking up, she went back to bed, curled up and started crying not knowing how her life could get so empty. She needed help. She needed answers.

# Chapter Four

## Walter Smith Gets Answers in the Desert

Walter Smith and the old man walked alone side by side through the empty desert. The leathery, grizzled old man was surprising in his brisk stride. Even Walter Smith's thirty-eight year old body was panting to keep up with him. The dirt road they walked on was plowed into the featureless desert spotted with occasional shrubs and the round fence without corners that encircled the site formed a horizon around them. There were some abandoned trucks and construction vehicles parked on the side of the road but the old man kept walking not noticing them. His old black eyes were fixed on the round metal structure looming ahead.

"Where do you think everyone's gone?" Walter Smith asked the old man. "You think it's some kind of holiday?" Walter was the type that couldn't deal with a lapse in conversation.

"You don't know where these people went?" The old man seemed suspicious that Walter Smith really didn't know what was going on. "You got no clue?"

"I suppose that you know what's going on?" Walter Smith said skeptically.

"Yep, space aliens got 'em," The old man said it matter-of-factly like it happens all the time. "...yep, got 'em all."

Walter Smith started laughing out loud and had no doubt that this old man sees space aliens all the time. After his laughter subsided, he could see that the old man's face was stern and serious. The look was so serious it made Walter nervous because it was obvious that at best this old guy had a mental problem of some sort. "You're joking right?" Walter asked.

"Nope, aliens got 'em. That's their ship over there." He pointed to the round silver structure they were approaching. It looked like a flying saucer, round and metallic with a generally flat disc shape. As they got closer its true size started to become apparent. It was two football fields across and four stories high.

Walter Smith's expression was held incredulous by the straightforward way this old man told such an obvious fantasy. "Wait, wait," Walter Smith said stopping the pace. "You expect me to believe that's a flying saucer? That's just part of the facility here … It's a particle accelerator. The 'super conducting supercollider' is what they call it."

"Nope, it's a flying saucer." The old man spoke like a tour guide. "The collider facility's all underground, shielded from cosmic rays."

"So aliens are here to steal the supercollider?" Walter Smith asked. "You know I saw a movie once where aliens from another dimension used a nuclear reactor to open a portal to our planet and launch an invasion." The old man actually reminded Walter of a trip he took to Seattle where he saw a ranting street vagrant claiming to own the Space Needle, accosting tourists and demanding his property rights. "... or maybe they've come to sabotage this thing!" At this point, he was just humoring the old man and remained focused on his mission to deliver toilet paper to the collider construction site.

"Nobody gives a shit about any supercollider. It isn't any more real than anything else here." the old man sneered at the desert. "But it's just the kind of place in the desert that people expect a UFO to land ... makes it easy to be here."

"You sure seem to know a lot about aliens," Walter said as they resumed they're pace down the road. Walking up to the round metallic structure he could see no details, the featureless metal had no screws, bolts, or welding. The shape was classic flying saucer shape like two plates put face to face forming a sharp edge. On the top was a dome also featureless with no windows or doors visible. "I'm sure you probably don't know so much about telephones around here, old man," Walter chided.

"Well ... I'll be honest with you." The old man looked down for a minute. After gathering strength to make a revelation he said, "I'm a space alien and I don't particularly need a phone."

Walter wasn't even phased by the statement. It was just the sort of thing he would expect to hear from an old man wandering alone in the desert, especially an old man that

86

thought that the supercollider was going to fly away to another planet.

The old man became indignant at Walter Smith's indifference to his admission. "You don't believe me, do you young fella?"

"Of course, I don't. There's no such thing as flying saucers ... Space aliens aren't real!"

"Now, that's mighty big talk from some asshole wandering lost in the desert with just some rolls of toilet paper to his name." the old man spoke like he'd been challenged to a duel. "What do you know about what's real. You could wake up back in your bed right now to find out all this is just a dream. You never know you're dreaming till you wake up." The man's tone turned malevolent. "… and then, it's too late."

"I know when I'm dreaming," Walter said resolutely. "My senses give me testable data that can be measured and …"

"Ha!" the old man shot back. "Your senses only mess you up more and don't have anywhere near the capacity to really know anything around you. Didn't you ever hear the old story of the blind guy and the elephant? When you got the elephant's tail you think it's a rope, you get its leg and thinks it's a tree, you get its trunk and think it's a snake. You get the tusk you think it's a bull and holding its floppy leathery ears makes you think it's got wings." The old man had to stop and laugh. "Not only have you got no clue what your looking at, but that piece of rope your holding is about to crap huge steaming elephant turds all over you."

"Oh, and how's that?" Walter asked. He didn't appreciate the imagery and didn't get the point.

"What if I'm the one dreaming about you and when I wake up back in bed you'll be gone." the old man said knowingly.

"What are you going to do? Blast me with your ray gun?" Walter replied laughing at the seemingly harmless old man trying not to think about a psychotic serial murderer vagrant.

"Is that what you want? You want me to blast you with my ray gun?" His intense stare told Walter that the old man actually did have a ray gun. "Is that what you want?"

"Uh well ..." Walter stammered as the comforting perception of a harmless old man was slipping from his mind. Clinging desperately to that perception he tried to change the tack of the conversation. "If you're an alien, what planet are you from?"

"You just don't get it son do you? There's no such thing as planets and stars and all that crap. You don't even know what's real much less where you are. How can you expect to understand where we come from?" The old man smacked his lips and slithered his tongue around the inside of his mouth as if he were clearing the taste of the fine dust they were breathing. His leather face and black eyes assessed Walter Smith's confusion. "You people, your

89

planets, your stars, everything about you ceases to exist at some point.  Over time all proof that any of you ever existed vanishes without a trace like you never existed. Something that can stop existing never really existed in the first place."

"Uh right."  Walter Smith was caught off guard by the old man's metaphysical rhetoric.  It was more sentences then the old man had spoke at once since they first met.  He had been expecting a simple answer like 'Mars' or 'Jupiter'.  "So you aliens are from some non-reality?" Walter asked.

"No, you people are from non-reality.  We're the only real thing in your world."

"... and you've kidnapped people of earth for some purpose or experiment?"  The old man's sci-fi delusion was interesting but Walter Smith still had a job to do. Somewhere there were earth people that needed toilet paper and he had to find them.  He was looking around for someone real while he spoke to the old man.

"A few were used in genetic experiments and some were used in attempts to heighten awareness of our existence so we can be here but most of them are just hidden."  The old man continued to speak as Walter snooped around the metal structure looking for a means to signal somebody, an intercom or doorbell.  "Are you listening to me son?"

"Yes, yes, you're holding thousands of earth people."  Walter was totally absorbed in the task of penetrating this facility and completing his delivery.  He studied massive structure then looked up and down the horizon paying no attention to the old man.

"We're not really holding them they're just somewhere else.  Turning a corner, going up the stairs or getting on an elevator, they're always somewhere other than here.  It's simply a fluke of your perception that if a person isn't in you're presence they no longer exist for you.  We can't do anything physically but nothing could make us more real then to make a bunch of people disappear ... even if they ain't really gone ..."

"Well, I'm sorry old timer but I got a job to do," Walter interrupted becoming concerned that he may not find anyone. "There's got to be someone in charge around here."

"Now, I got you thinking about aliens, didn't I?" The old man said it like he had completed his mission. "Every flying saucer you ever saw you figgered was some kind of shooting star or satellite or something. There are a lot of people like you out there. We can hover right over their house and they think it's some government experiment. Your kind are so wrapped up in your own fantasy world that we couldn't get close to you or anything around you. Even standing in front of this giant flying saucer you don't see it!"

"No I don't. I don't see any UFOs or aliens just a crazy old man." Walter openly declared.

"But, you're thinking about it," The old man said with a gleam in his eye. "You're thinking about aliens and right now if I showed you one you'd probably believe it ... Am I right? And since it's just the two of us all alone out here, if I was an alien you couldn't do much about it. Could you?"

"Yeah old man, show me an alien."

"Are you sure?" The old man lowered his voice and brought his face closer to Walter Smith. "If I show you an alien now you're gonna know it's real."

"Yeah sure," Walter said. The breeze stilled and everything got quiet.

"You're sure?"

"Sure." Walter said not backing away from the old man's proximity. "Show me an alien," he said resolutely.

"Okay, you asked for it." The old man reached over his head and grabbed the back of his own neck. Then like a secret agent in an old movie tearing off his disguise, he peeled off his face revealing a horribly different face and head. His small hairless head was covered with gray skin that was dimpled like the skin of an orange. He had no nose only nostrils and a mouth without lips. The eyes were almond shaped eggs of black glass. The old man with the new face lunged at Walter Smith.

Walter fell back on to the ground screaming and yelling as the old man came at him hissing and waving his arms. He tried repeatedly to get back to his feet but panic kept him falling and stumbling on all fours as he scrambled away from the horrific face. It felt like he was moving and thrashing in slow motion not getting anywhere but finally, he made it to his feet and left at a dead run. Behind him he could hear the old man's laughter wafting through the air like the clouds of dust he kicked up.

"You'd better run!" the old man yelled after him amidst laughter. "I'll blast you with my ray gun!" he bellowed with renewed laughter at his own joke as he watched

Walter Smith run off into the desert.

# Chapter Five

## Dr. Carter's Sister is Missing

Cassie burst out of the door to the meeting room at a dead run fighting back tears and struggling to keep her breathing regular. She shoved passed people on their way into the room spilling her papers but not giving them a look back as she fled. Her terror was only boosted by the embarrassment she felt at the spectacle she was. Others in the hallway looked at her and couldn't help but think, "What the hell is her problem?"

There was no way she could stand around with those people waiting for an elevator so she ran directly to the door to the stairwell. Her terrified footfalls echoed down the empty stairway. The emptiness of the stairs gave her comfort at being alone away from people but also the fear from being alone. She ran down two flights and exploded through a door to the underground parking garage where her car was parked.

Her shiny Jaguar sports coupe was no comfort until she got inside and locked the door. The solid clunk of the door closing sealed out the rest of the world and there was peace. Only the sound of her sobbing filled the car. She sat there crying replaying the whole incident in her head over and over again trying to convince herself that it didn't really happen. Maybe it was just another anxiety dream about strange little people and she would wake up back in her bed. But the harsh reality of the underground parking garage wouldn't fade. It really happened.

Cassie had given speeches and presentations before sometimes in front of hundreds of people but nothing like this had ever happened. She had always enjoyed being the center of attention but as she went up to the podium before the city planning commission to ask for a variance in local zoning, she felt tension welling up in the pit of her stomach. There were only twelve people seated in a semicircle facing her but they were all stone face and the round shape of the room seemed to focus on her. City commissioner Bovar was seated on the end. He was the one who was always trying to get glimpses up or down her dress and the way he looked at her always made her feel like she wasn't wearing a dress at all.

She could have asked to do her presentation another day but she was sure she could keep it under control and the SMS deal was already in trouble. Still the roundness of the room and the cool white light of the concealed lighting haunted her and she could feel other eyes besides the committee upon her. They were sneaky eyes peeking around the corner. She got up to the podium and stole looks around the room trying to catch someone else looking at her but she saw only the committee and they were exchanging looks amongst themselves trying to understand Cassie's paranoid shiftiness. She was shaking as she fumbled through papers and began to speak.

"Esteemed committee members," she started but her voice cracked and she started over. "The code variance I'm asking for is …" Again she stopped to stare at the emotionless faces looking at her. Why were they so cold? Why were they doing this to her? In the corner of her eye she saw someone peek at her from coat closet and quickly close the door. Her rational mind told her that there was no one in the closet so she forced herself to continue speaking. "Supply Management Services is a national warehousing and distribution operation that could bring over one hundred full time jobs to this area ..." She stopped when she realized that she had started reading in the middle of the page skipping her opening paragraph and leaving the committee with confused looks. The only emotion she had yet seen in their faces. Commissioner Bovar seemed almost turned on by her vulnerability and it made her skin tightened down her back. Her stomach was knotting and her heart began to race and flutter but she had too much riding on this deal to stop now.

"I'm seeking a minor variance in code to allow ..." She was now completely unnerved by the skeptical looks going around the room and there was again someone staring at her from the closet. It was someone short like a child with large eyes that could see through her clothes. She whipped around just in time to see the closet quickly close. She started panting as she could feel their eyes probing her. "I'm needing ..." Her words were broken by more panting. "I ..."

Finally, Cassie could no longer take it and she was going to catch that little son of a bitch in the closet. She left the podium, ran to the closet and violently flung the door open. A skeletal empty coat rack fell out of the empty closet on to the floor in front of her. Cassie jumped back screaming at the top of her lungs as if a dead body had fallen in front of her. She screamed and screamed at the motionless coat rack while some of the committee members rose in concern and tried to approach her.

She stopped midscream with a gasp that nearly gagged her and whipped around with an insane look that froze everybody in the room. One of the committee members had a telephone handset in his hand as if he were about to call for help. Everyone stood motionless waiting to see what her next move would be. There was a sigh of relief as she simply burst into tears and fled the room.

Cassie sat in her car for almost five full minutes before she could finally stop crying and get her breathing back under control.  Once the adrenaline of fear and self loathing

passed she realized what this had cost her.  Not only were

thousands of dollars worth of surveys and appraisal work

scattered all up and down the hallways but there was no

way anybody would ever do business with her again.  Now

her eyes burned from tears, her nose was clogged and she

was getting a headache in the middle of her forehead but

she was finally starting to relax.  The garage was full of

cars but no people to see her torment.

Across the driveway, she saw one car that caught her

attention.  It was a large gray four door from the late

seventies that was completely dinghy and drab except for a

neon green bumper sticker with black type and a cartoon

face.  It read "Take me to your reefer!" and a cartoon face

depicted the stereotypical space alien with a large head and

black almond shaped eyes.  This alien had a mischievous

look and a hand rolled joint hanging from his lips.  It was

looking at her.

The memories of that face came back to her in waves. She knew the memories had been there but she kept them tucked away in an unreality dream state. The images were so unreal that it was easy to believe that it didn't happen but the details of the texture and color of their skin, the empty black eyes were burned permanently into her mind. How could she ever deny the things they did to her? As she remembered the horror she realized how long it had been following her and she couldn't imagine her life without it.

She sat with her vision locked on the little cartoon face on the bumper sticker. Her breath was short exhalations unable to inhale completely for a scream. The breath wouldn't come, the face had paralyzed her with fear and it was a familiar feeling. A warm dampness spread in her seat breaking the nightmare, she had wet herself. The alien face was snickering at her.

Cassie fumbled with her cellular phone about to dial nine, one, one but stopped. She couldn't dial 911 about aliens. They'd think she's crazy. That gave her a different idea and she dialed again.

"Dr. Carter's office," a new alert phone voice answered. "May I help you?"

"Yes ..." Cassie tried to hold back her tears at least long enough to deal with the secretary. "Is Dr. Carter available?"

"Yes, in fact she was just finishing for the day. I'll connect you." In the moment of electronic silence she sat waiting struggling to keep her mind still so the thoughts could come back. The familiar voice that had helped Cassie through so much came on. "This is Dr. Carter."

"Oh Doctor." Just the calm sound of the Doctor's voice put a more rational spin on her world and suddenly Cassie didn't know what to tell the Doctor. "Doctor ... I've had some kind of anxiety attack. I'm not sure," she said tentatively.

"Cassie where are you? Are you safe?" the Doctor asked an urgent but calm telephone voice.

"Yes, I think. I don't know." Cassie had shared everything with this woman but still couldn't bring herself to tell her what this was really about.

"Cassie?" It was obvious to Dr. Carter that Cassie was holding something back, something she desperately wanted to talk about. "Cassie, what brought this on? Did it have anything to do with your nightmares?"

While Dr. Carter spoke Cassie's mind was again captured by the little face on the bumper sticker. The alien almond eyes knew all about her. They probed her over and over in every way and they would be back. "Doctor ... I think but it can't ..." Tears filled her eyes and washed the face out of her vision only then could she cry the words,

"They're not real people ... They're not real people. They take me at night ..."

"Cassie? Cassie, where do they take you at night?" Dr. Carter could transmit her therapeutic voice over the phone and it brought Cassie into the safe state of mind that she felt in the Doctor's office. "Cassie, tell me what you can."

"They took me to a ship... a UFO!" The recollection released a wall of pent up emotional tears and words pouring out of her. "They took off my clothes, they held me down, I couldn't move. They did things to me." Her broken sentences finally collapsed into full crying.

"Cassie, can you come see me? I was about to leave for the day but I can wait for you."

"Yes, yes. I'm in the parking garage at the downtown city hall annex. I can be there in ten minutes."

"Perfect, I think I know what's happening to you."

Cassie hung up the phone and dug up a gym bag in the backseat with a set of gray warm up clothes in it. She squirmed around changing clothes there in the car and used her expensive outfit to mop up the drivers seat. Catching a glimpse of herself in the mirror she was shocked by what she had become. She walked into the building a well dressed real estate executive now she was in a frumpy and floppy gray sweat suit with her business ruined. Her hair was a neat bun centered on the top of her head now fell to one side with a few delinquent tresses sticking out in different directions. Her make-up was smudged and smeared on her tear swollen face. Something had happened to her.

Cassie poked her head into Dr. Carter's office to see Doctor Carter slumped behind her large desk with her face in her hands.

"Doctor, are you okay?" Cassie said gently as she slipped quietly into the office.

The Doctor looked up startled but relaxed with a weary smile when she saw who it was. "I'm sorry?" she said. "Please come in." Her voice was shaky and even her powerful professionalism couldn't hide that something painful had just happened.

"What's going on?" Cassie asked as she eased up and sat on the couch wide eyed at the sight of her mentor so visibly shaken.

"Well, I have a sister that lives in Colorado ... in a suburb of Colorado Springs." The Doctor stopped speaking for a moment struggling with the idea of telling Cassie the story. It was too late to turn back so she went on. "She's got a five year old that's been missing for three days. They think he wandered off into the woods near their house and got lost. It's in the Rocky Mountains and the country's pretty rugged. They've had search parties with dogs and helicopters for days. But today ... I just got a call." Her voice slowed to a stop as if she were out of breath.

"Did they ... find him?" Cassie asked but she sensed that the end to the story was not a happy one.

"No ..." the Doctor said skipping a breath. "Last night my sister vanished. The police say she probably went out on her own in the middle of the night to find her son in the wilderness."

Cassie was engrossed in the Doctor's story and silently mouthed the words, "oh God."

"I talked to her just yesterday and the guilt was killing her. She said she only turned her back for a minute and he was gone." Dr. Carter had to stop talking for a pause to keep from crying. "She didn't leave a note or tell anyone."

"Oh I'm so sorry," Cassie said as she came over to kneel next to the Doctor's chair and hug her. "I know how it feels." Cassie let go of the hug and said intimately, "I have a friend, Tina, who's been missing for a week. She was the only close friend I had. We filed missing persons reports but there's just nothing. She's gone. I've been calling the police every day." Cassie stopped talking and an awkward silence fell on them both. Pain was settling around them like falling snow. Something occurred to Cassie and she finally spoke. "Isn't it strange… that we would both know people disappeared? … almost at the same time? What's happening here?"

"Oh Cassie, no." The Doctor looked deep into Cassie tried to comfort her from within. "We can't give circumstance anything more than it deserves. Seeing patterns in coincidence is just a type of hallucination."

Cassie had been listening empathetically but something on the Doctor's desk caught her attention and held her spellbound. A psychiatry journal was open to a page with a picture of a crude hand drawn sketch of a face. It was the same large headed, almond eyed face that she had seen so many times under bright white lights and shiny metal surfaces. After a few seconds, Cassie realized that she was staring without breathing. The crude drawing had paralyzed her and she couldn't breathe or move.

Cassie's fear melted away Dr. Carter's stress. "Cassie, do you recognize this drawing? This is part of what I wanted to show you," the Doctor asked entranced by Cassie's reaction to the picture.

Cassie was so enthralled by the sketch that it took her a moment to compose herself. "Yes, yes, those are the faces in my dreams. Who drew this?"

"A woman in California, she has nightmares about these people taking her away several times a week." the Doctor said closely watching Cassie. "She says that they come in flying saucers, paralyze her and subject her to all kinds of medical tests. We're seeing more and more of these cases reported in the medical literature."

Cassie's face went blank. She knew the story all too well even though she really didn't remember it. She could picture the bright lights, stainless steel tools and the horrible inhuman faces. "This is really happening. We are being attacked." Cassie exhaled the words in shock.

"Well Cassie, reality is relative. Whether or not it's real it's affecting your life and the lives of others."

"Others?" Cassie finally broke her vision from the drawing back to the Doctor.

"Yes," the Doctor pulled another drawing out of a manila folder. It was the same type of crude drawing of the almond-eyed face perched on skinny spindly body. "This one was drawn by a man in Iowa ... and let me show you this ..." She pulled a textbook off her shelf entitled 'Abnormal Psychology' and opened it to a page she had marked. The marked page had photos of similar drawings. "These were drawn by a chieftain of an indigenous tribe isolated in the Amazon basin."

"So this is really happening ... happening to other people all over the world?" Cassie thought it would comfort her to find out that she wasn't going insane but instead she was frightened. There was something terrible happening all over the world.

"It is really happening ... but," Dr. Carter paused delicately. "There are no aliens, no flying saucers."

"But how? If other people are seeing the same things I'm seeing, this has to be real. How can it not be?"

"It is real, Cassie. The pain is real, the lives being destroyed are real but nothing beyond the symptoms is real," the Doctor said compassionately trying to soothe Cassie's confused look. "The woman who drew this 'alien' says that she met the reanimated corpse of Elvis Presley on board a flying saucer and now she even sings duets with him during her extraterrestrial visits. The man from Iowa claims that the aliens force him to have sex with unconscious TV and movie stars. The celebrities are of course unaware that they are being abducted nightly to participate in this man's episodes."

"So these people are crazy and I'm one of them." Cassie's mind started to build a new realization. "These dreams, these attacks, I am going insane."

"Cassie, people manifest stress and psychological problems in a lot of ways. Sometimes our minds give that stress a form and character all its own. Your stress, like their stress, simply took on the form of hostile aliens. It happens to a lot of people."

"Apparently, it even happens to Amazon chieftains," Cassie said looking at the picture in the textbook.

"Those people in the Amazon didn't even know about other planets, much less people from other planets until five years ago. That's when a logging company talked them into trading logging rights on some of their land for a satellite dish and color TV for their village meeting hall. Prior to the arrival of TV, there had been a few dragons, some demons and spirits but never one flying saucer in five thousand years of their oral history. This alien face and its stories are spread all over the world from mind to mind."

"But I'm going crazy and you want to tell me that my subconscious latched on to some cultural icon to manifest ..." Cassie was getting almost panicked; the office was closing in on her again. Emotionally, she had to back delicately away from the subject like a ticking bomb. "How do I make it stop?" she pleaded.

"Cassie, remember what your life was like when you first came to me five years ago? You were afraid of everything, having nightmares, anxiety attacks. These are just the type of things that victims of violence and trauma have to cope with. Do you remember people peeking at you wanting to tear your clothes off and hurt you just like these people?" The Doctor stopped to check Cassie's breathing then continued reassuringly. "Right now, your stress disorder manifests itself mainly in your sleep but it's starting to affect your unconscious waking mind. If you don't change your lifestyle next it will affect your conscience waking mind and then you'll be singing with Elvis ... or worse.  But we both know that's not going to happen. Right?"

"Right.  Because I'll start coming to you once a week, and take some time off." Cassie recited as if she were the Doctor.  Her humor was a feeble attempt to show the Doctor she was okay.

"Don't smoke, drink only in moderation and pay the secretary on the way out." The Doctor added jokingly.  "Cassie, there's nothing crazy about you.  What's going on inside your head is no different than any phobia or a compulsive behavior.  I just read a study that showed survivors of trauma are statistically much more likely to see ghosts or flying saucers than the general population."

"Oh great, now ghosts," Cassie said dejectedly.

"Actually the term was 'paranormal phenomenon' and the way you push yourself  it's surprising that you don't have flying saucers, poltergeists, chupa cabres and loch ness monsters all at the same time. Cassie you've got to get the message and slow down."

Cassie was driving home that night thinking about what the Doctor had said. The nightmares and anxiety attacks could deteriorate into a full dementia if she let it. But she didn't know how to live when she wasn't buried in work. As long as there was work she didn't have to think about the past, future or her feelings; just deals to make, paperwork and meetings. Especially now with Tina gone and no one else in her life, a day off meant just sitting at home with nothing to do.

Cassie jerked physically startled to realize that she didn't remember the last few minutes of driving like she had nodded off and just woke up. She was so absorbed in thought that she didn't even remember leaving the Doctor's office. Even more startling she realized it was really dark for so early in the evening. Instead of six forty-five it was eight forty-five. While driving, she tried mentally to reconstruct the evening and account for the extra two hours but couldn't. Losing time was a symptom of some stress related psychological disorders but there was something else haunting her. Her car was alone on the normally busy Parker Road. This particular stretch of road was isolated as it looped around the outskirts of town but it was never empty like this. She noticed a single bright star crawling across the night sky paralleling her course and when she looked directly at the star it stopped moving and started coming directly at her.

Cassie sensed something sinister about the star and could have stomped the accelerator pedal to the floor but the idea of running away would never occur to her. There was no place on the whole planet to hide from these people. Her mind was the beacon they would navigate by and it would always lead them to her. She didn't even have to fall asleep; they were in her waking life and couldn't or wouldn't be removed. They were everywhere she was and could walk through walls, control her body and read her thoughts. Suddenly the car's engine died and all the dashboard lights went out leaving Cassie coasting quietly in the dark. She stopped her car in the middle of the empty road and got out to stand in the street.

The dense silence of the night held her spellbound. There was no traffic noise, no airplanes and no sounds coming from the city. There weren't even any natural sounds like breezes, crickets or barking dogs, just utter quiet. It was something that UFO abductees called the 'Oz Factor', a feeling of isolation in a place that was normally crowded with people and activity. She had heard the Doctor use the term but she didn't remember that part of the conversation. There was a flash of light and Cassie was gone. Her car sitting alone in the dark suddenly started back up on its own and sat idling quietly with the driver's door still open.

Cassie found herself laid out flat on a low metal table. The cold metal table surface on her skin, the lights and every other detail had been specifically created to make it real to her. That way, it didn't matter if she was struggling to awaken from a nightmare or awaken to a nightmare. In one life, her career was destroyed, by now her properties and possessions had been considered abandoned. Tanya would keep the office running as long as she could but when payday rolled around and Cassie still didn't show up with the paychecks, Tanya wouldn't come back. Cassie's Jaguar was parked idling in the road until the police towed it away. Everyone and everything she knew was gone. In another life, two aliens took her feet and spread her legs while a third took a position between them with the bladed device. No matter which was real the horror of either existence didn't matter anymore. Exhaustion overtook her and she fell asleep.

"Cassandra!" A voice pierced Cassie's fatigue pulling her from a blackout sleep. She felt like she had been asleep for weeks. "Cassandra Vega, you wake yourself this instant." The stern commanding voice sent a chill down her spine that was distantly familiar. It could reach her in a way they could no longer reach with torture and little gray monsters. "This is why you fail my class and this is why you will always fail at everything you do." The flat round lenses of his wire rimmed glasses were mirrors under the brilliant white lights hiding his eyes but his black pointed goat tee could make anyone look satanic.

In terror, Cassie realized that she was back in her junior year of college in Professor Kroner's logic class and she had fallen asleep at her desk in front of everyone. Worse yet, she couldn't wake up and even with all her strength she could barely open her eyes which still rolled back in her head. Of all the classes and all the professors in the university, falling asleep in Professor Kroner's class was every student's nightmare. He wouldn't just fail a student which meant the student would face him again next semester. He would verbally abuse them in front of the entire class for ten minutes before telling them that they were out of the class. Wrong answers spoken in class were punished by personal attacks that sometimes led to tears. UFOs and aliens could be imaginary but the terror of Professor Kroner was undeniably real.

"You see ..." Professor Kroner said smugly. "You can't even focus your own awareness." Cassie couldn't see anything but like a dream she just knew what was going on around her. She was naked on her back on a metal table in the middle of a round auditorium. The professor walked around her speaking as if he was lecturing a class and Cassie was the display. "Cassandra Vega," he continued. "Our problem, and it is your problem too, is that we can bring you here and you can bring us there but without a standard of reality here and there doesn't matter."

In her mind, she could see the huge round auditorium high atop a tower looking over a glowing city and the same giant round structure floating a few feet off the ground in the Texas desert. There were smaller versions of odd shapes and colors darting around the sky over the rest of the United States. They were all the same place. A frightened little girl in the back of her mind shouted, "Why don't you go back to outer space and leave earth alone!"

The professor laughed demonically and said, "You have no real understanding of what's happening here! Nobody cares about your round little planet or its round little people shitting round little turds to swirl down round toilets." He hesitated as something funny occurred to him. "In fact, we're not coming from outer space to invade earth. We're coming from earth to invade outer space!" With that, he burst into another torrent of evil laughter.

"Why do you want me?" A different voice in her head cried out in catharsis. "Why don't you leave me alone?"

"Oh we need you. We need you to know that we are here," the professor explained grandly as he walked around the table. "Without your awareness, we don't exist here. We've tried everything, anything that could give us a physical presence here. You know, it was very easy to capture the awareness of your beef cattle; cows would simply stand there staring off into space while we dissected them. Unfortunately, they knew nothing beyond themselves and couldn't go anywhere. We've even tried to combine our bodies with yours on the genetic level bridging the gap during the egg phase of your short lives. The resulting fetuses were very unstable. All reality is always crippled by doubt."

Cassie saw in her mind all the cattle mutilations and UFO stories where women were taken on flying saucers and had their eggs harvested. It was a very specific agenda to promote their existence which was locked out by paradox. The people here would only be aware of them if they existed but they needed that awareness in the first place to exist here. The optical illusion of our cosmos' infinitude was drawing them here as if their own infinite world wasn't enough. She could almost understand what was going on. She could almost know what it was like to look out over a flat horizon instead of a round horizon. The curve of the earth's horizon became visibly obvious after looking at the flat horizon long enough.

"Now Cassie," the professor interrupted her thoughts. "It's time for us to begin." The professor walked out and three of the small gray people took his place at the table side. They wanted her total and acute awareness and they wanted to see how far that awareness could reach out. She had always been an outsider and those desolate feelings gave them a big head start as their flying saucer traveled in the emptiness. Cassie saw blue sky between her and the ground then the blue sky turned to night and stars became visible. The earth fell away beneath her and became a bright star in a faraway sky. Everything she knew was shrinking in the distance as they carried her away.

The passing stars began to look alike and started to slow to a crawl. The aliens knew that they needed to intensify her experience of them and they gathered around her. Their intimidating stares were usually enough to frighten a human into heightened awareness but Cassie had been through it so much that it didn't affect her any more. One alien produced some stainless steel hand held device with prongs and blades all over it. It looked like a cross between a medieval torture tool and a gynecological instrument. It had no purpose but to bring pain and fear just like all the appliances they had used on her.

There was nothing they could do to her that they hadn't already done before but Cassie's mind still shrank involuntarily at the memory of how the device was used. She now remembered everything and it reminded her of horrific stories from surgical patients who regained consciousness during surgery but were still paralyzed by the anesthetic. They could only lie there fully awake through hours of surgery feeling the pain of every incision and the surgeon hands in their bodies. The experience usually left them mentally shattered for years with all the same symptoms Cassie had. But Cassie had gotten used to it, they couldn't hurt her anymore. The passing stars stopped.

One of the aliens put his face nose to nose with hers. He hissed angrily and crinkled the gray dimply skin where his nose should have been but Cassie looked past him vacantly. He reached up with a three finger hand and started to squeeze and jostle her face but she laid there unresponsive like a rag doll. "Bah!" the alien snorted both telepathically and verbally then stomped out in frustration. The others followed him out of the room leaving her totally alone. Just like a dream that seemed hours long in a few moments, a split second was ten thousand years of loneliness and her mind cried out for her tormentors to return. They left her alone for eons unable to move with no one but herself.

Cassie had won. She knew that she would never leave this place but she still won. There would be no heroic rescue by some handsome well built army guy but at least they couldn't hurt her anymore. In reality, they held thousands of heroic army guys in little boxes walking around completely unaware that they were really inside of a glowing booth stacked with hundreds of thousands, now millions of other glowing booths. Like a monolith of little TVs each glowing screen showed another person lost in thought during some mindless activity. Now that Cassie was useless to them she knew she would be put in a box and her disappearance would impact the lives of others who would also get caught up in this.

There was no stopping what was happening around her but she had still won. It was a small victory almost unnoticed but it meant that she had mastered the little bubble of reality within herself. Someone else mastered the bubble of reality around her and the concentric bubbles formed by the police, the army, the government, and the world. They were all walking around happily in their fantasy but Cassie was cursed with the knowledge of where she was. Once she woke up and glimpsed reality she couldn't go back to sleep no matter how sweet the dreams were.

Cassie barely noticed the five year old little girl with brown hair standing at her tableside. The little girl was a soul created in the same place where all the inhabitants of dreams are born. Cassie knew it was just another part of herself trapped here, just a daydream made flesh by a desperate mind alone in the void. "Why are you so sad?" the little girl asked with caring, inquisitive eyes.

The little brunette moppet brightened Cassie enough for a weak smile. Cassie said gently. "I'm sad because these bad people brought me here."

"Oh," the little girl answered. She seemed satisfied for a moment but like a child, her mind kept processing. "But why did they bring us here?" she asked restlessly.

Cassie struggled to come up with an answer that a child could relate to. She was seeing a side of herself she had long forgotten when she had brown hair that would get darker the rest of her life. Finally, she said, "They want to take everything we have…the sky, the trees, our friends, love, everything. They want everything…" Cassie trailed off and let the little girl fade into the shadows.

The little girl instinctively wanted to make the sad lady feel better. She reached up on the table and put her hand on Cassie's shoulder. "Do you want to know a secret?" she said mischievously. "I'm really a princess."

The little girl's confession caught Cassie off guard and she had to smile as she looked into the bright young face. When did she ever lose that childhood imagination and hope? Cassie had no control over the environment in her head but this little girl was Supreme Being in hers. "So where's your castle?" Cassie asked wanting to escape back into that childhood fantasy world. "What's it like?"

"Oh, it's far away from here," the little girl said importantly and informatively. "But there's ponies and dogs and cats. All kinds of people live there like my Smurfs and my Beanie Babies. We play there all the time."

"It sounds like a great place," Cassie said sniffing back a tear. This little girl's mind imposed its own design on the world around her. Cassie, for all her age, wisdom and education was at the mercy of a world imposing its design on her mind.

"You can ask Barbie. She lives there." The little girl produced a Barbie doll just over a foot tall with long blond hair and held it up like a candle. "...and do you know what else? She's married. She has a husband," the child said giggling shyly.

"What's her husband's name?" Cassie asked remembering how she reenacted grand weddings with her toy dolls. It was a dream brought to life by little girls countless times over the generations.

"His name is G.I.Joe. He's a little taller than Barbie and he has real hair that's fuzzy. He's an army soldier like daddy," the little girl explained. "He's coming to rescue us and take us back to the kingdom so he and Barbie can live happily ever after."

"I'm afraid that's not going to happen." Professor Kroner stepped forward from the shadows. "You're a very special little girl and you're coming with me."

"Why?" the little girl asked clutching her Barbie closely.

"Because taking you will hurt Cassandra Vega." The Professor bent down to explain sweetly to the child. "You're really all that's left of her." He straightened up to address Cassie laid on the table. "It's going to get worse yet Cassandra Vega. You will eventually be reduced to an

132

infant not just at my mercy but dependent on me for your very existence. We will milk your awareness like a helpless dairy cow for all of eternity. You should find it a small price to pay for immortality." He gave Cassie one more smirk before he said to the little girl, "Okay, take my hand... OH look a Barbie doll, Isn't that precious. May I hold her?" he asked sinisterly. Cassie could only watch helplessly while the evil being toyed with the child.

"Okay," the little girl said reluctantly handing over the doll. "But her husband, G.I. Joe is coming and he's real"

"Of course, he's real. Just like Barbie..." the professor said mockingly and revealing to Cassie that the doll he held was now a living breathing woman reduced to just over a foot tall. The woman shrieked in terror at the giant satanic face of the professor peering at her through his round glasses while he gripped her like King Kong holding Faye Wray. Her tiny screams of utter horror and begging for help made Cassie sick to her stomach but they could force her to watch him brutalizing the small blonde woman. He stripped off the small pink prom dress revealing the tiny details of her nudity while she writhed and pleaded for her life. "If I was only a few feet shorter," the professor said looking at the tiny woman like a morsel of food. He repeatedly thumped the tiny face by flicking it with the back of his forefinger crushing the woman's features beyond recognition with splatters of blood. Finally as the woman's screams fell to sobs, he crushed her head like a blood filled grape with a crunch that they made sure Cassie could hear.

Cassie was allowed to lean over the edge of the table to see the diminutive bloody corpse that he dropped on the floor. It was like looking at the decapitated body of a woman on the sidewalk from a tall building above. It was someone who had been brought here just like she had been or someone missing who was like Tina. A puddle of blood was getting larger around the body and Cassie started to shake, unable to drive the gory image out of her head. She felt herself starting to go into shock as her heart started to race, delighting the professor.

"It's okay lady," the little girl put a sensitive hand on Cassie's shoulder and leaned closer to the table. "She was just a doll." She said to Cassie confidentially looking down at the floor.

Cassie stared incredulously at the child's sweet calm face for a moment and it actually slowed her heart and calmed her breathing. Experiencing the look of innocence relaxed her and she leaned over the table to see the lifeless toy lying on the floor with its empty plastic head pushed in. She looked at it in disbelief trying to reconcile what she thought she saw to what she was seeing now. Suddenly, the resilient plastic face popped back into shape causing the doll to jump slightly, startling Cassie. It lay there unharmed smiling for a beauty pageant as the little girl reclaimed it.

"You should go home now," the little girl said to Professor Kroner delicately. "G.I. Joe is going to be really upset about what you did to Barbie."

"Really?" the Professor said with mock concern stooping down to the child. "You might be right. We'd better go look for him. Cassandra Vega will stay here and watch what happens to G.I.Joe when we find him."

# Chapter Six

## The General and the Dominatrix

Pulling his collar up against the elements as he got out of his car, the General stopped to look up at the silhouette of the grand old house against the stormy night sky. He didn't notice the silhouette of the little girl and the bearded man with glasses in the shadowy hedge. All the windows of the house were dark or heavily shaded so no light escaped. It looked like a scene from a horror movie as he hustled up the walkway through the drizzle but he sensed the familiar warmth and comfort waiting inside. The house was a timeless bubble of reality all its own with clean rounded lines of experience closing back on themselves sealing another world within and repelling anything from outside.

The General came into the foyer of the large mansion shaking the night's drizzle off his trench coat before removing it. He was escaping his box of career and family but stopped here to tie up some loose ends before he turned his back on it all forever. He had gray hair and an intelligent chiseled face that could work as a military officer, a scientist, a cowboy or a grandfather. He wore a cardigan sweater over a dress shirt and a tie accenting his crisply pressed dressy slacks and shoes that looked like they were just shined minutes ago without a trace of the dirty weather outside on them.

The reception area had a large hardwood desk with a pretty young woman sitting behind it who greeted him as he approached. "Well, hello General! We haven't seen you in a while. Mistress Valerie was a little worried. You know we see these stories in the news lately ..."

"Oh I've been really busy lately but I'm okay," the General interrupted. "How've you been Elisa?" While the general spoke his face softened as it dawned on him that she was wearing a shear negligee revealing her entire body. The face that commanded respect and obedience from tens of thousands melted into a gentle smile at the site of the beautiful scantily clad young girl. She could see the tranquilizing effect she was having on him so she modeled for a moment.

"You know how things are here at 'La Chateau', same as they've always been since nineteen twenty nine, busy as ever," Elisa said. She had already surreptitiously pushed buttons on the intercom to let Mistress Valerie know someone was here to see her. "You're lucky to catch the Mistress unoccupied. Usually we're booked solid a week in advance. I think the East Discipline room is empty till two A.M. Would you like a cognac?"

"No, but thank you," the General declined. He had traveled all over the world and knew the service here to be some of the best. "I wouldn't think of showing up without a reservation if I wanted to book a session. I just have something to drop off for the Mistress. If she's not busy maybe you could tell her I'm here ..." The powerful General was becoming a schoolboy.

"She's in her office, she knows you're here and she'll see you now," Elisa said mysteriously looking at a light on a small switch board on the desk.

"Thank You," the General said as he went up the stairs. He spent most of his time with her in one of the dungeons but he knew where the office was. The Mistress would occasionally have visitors in her private office for personal lingerie shows or body piercing but it didn't have the equipment and room to move around that most of her clients wanted. In a hallway at the top of the stairs there was a bedroom converted into an office.

The General opened the door and found the room to be dimly lit by candles and overwhelmed by a large desk with a dark shadow of a woman sitting behind it. The woman touched the desk surface and slowly the lights came up to a comfortable level revealing Mistress Valerie: a tall slender black woman sitting at her desk like the CEO of a fortune five hundred company. Her long hair was done in tight beaded braids hanging to her shoulders and giving her a hooded silhouette in front of the stormy night through the closed curtains. She stood revealing that she wore a black leather corset, black panties, then sauntered around the desk to reveal high heeled black leather boots laced up passed the knee. The General could almost feel himself physically shrinking to the size of a twelve year old boy when he was near her.

"Good to see you, General," she said holding out her hand for a professional handshake. Her manner was business-like but perched up on the high heels she looked like a preying mantis as she reached out.

"I miss serving you," he said turning her hand up so he could kiss its back. He wanted to strip off his shirt and kneel down at her feet so her boots would tower over him and he could see up her legs to her crotch. "How've you been?" he asked.

"I've been well. We've had a couple of our ladies move on so we've been really busy." The Mistress stood there in the front of the desk allowing the General to take in her full dominatrix regalia. She watched his eyes following her legs up to her crotch where only a small patch of fabric from a black thong panty covered her. "I'm surprised to see you tonight ... Do you want to go downstairs?"

The General broke the trance that her panties held on him then looked down. "I just want to talk ..." His tone became subservient as he spoke. He could give her total control as he did two or three times a month for the last five years and all the pressure of who he was would become non-reality. Correcting himself, he added respectfully, "I just wanted to talk 'Mistress.'" In her presence, he had no responsibility except her approval. Simple unthinking obedience could earn him the privilege of rubbing oil on her feet or covering her dark naked body with lotion. If he pleased her enough she would allow him to masturbate in front of her while she showed him her breasts. Her discipline was just as delightful with bondage and whippings. "I probably won't see you anymore," he said dropping his shoulders like someone who just failed their family.

"You're one of my best hung submissives. Are you leaving?" The mistress led them over to sit on a garish red velvet sofa that had hardwood trim. She had always said it looked right at home in a whore house.

"Yes mistress, I'm leaving," the General said contritely. His submission as a five star general to this woman wasn't real. It was part of the role he played to escape the pressures of his world. But even in role play there was no denying the reality of being gagged and bound nude while the spike heel of the Mistress's boot stabbed into his buttock. The line between real and unreal was often blurred in their relationship and he loved the helpless powerless feeling so much that it was easy to lose himself in it all. It was a relaxing getaway for a powerful man.

"Speak freely," Mistress Valerie encouraged him. Their roles had been so entrenched over the years that the General found it hard to break out. But the Mistress sincerely cared about her customers and pressed him. "I want to know," she said with gentle but definite firmness.

"Things have been tough at work ... I'm leaving my job," the General confessed. "I can't deal with what's happening."

144

"How does an army general have a tough time at work?" she asked bewildered. "There's always a war going on somewhere." She had always imagined him giving orders that weren't questioned. She never thought or asked about what his responsibilities actually were.

"War is the easy part. We've got protocols and procedures. It's peacetime that we have problems with." The General's voice began to slow as her outfit recaptured his attention. "I'm resigning my commission ... quitting my job." He could see that she needed another translation. "I'm giving up my army career. I can't handle what's happening. I came to say goodbye," he said with a defeated voice.

"What's going on? What can't you handle?" Mistress Valerie could only imagine that the General had been caught up in some sex scandal or maybe his wife had found out about his membership at the dungeon. But if it was anything like that she would have seen something on the local news. She reasserted her role as mistress and spoke, "You know you can tell me ...You know you can tell me the things you can't tell anyone else. Nobody knows who I am." She was one person that powerful people told their secrets to and in exchange they protected her secrets.

"I sent twenty three hundred soldiers to vanish in the desert." the General finally said looking at the floor.

"General, if you're talking about troops in the Middle East, you know that it's part of the job. You've seen it before." What she knew of the General was that he was a war hero. She couldn't imagine what could be so bad in the face of all the horror and bloodshed he had seen over thirty-five years of war.

"No Mistress. It's not war. It's here in the states." The General hadn't stopped to put together the whole story in his head. This was the first time he talked to anyone about what was happening and he had to stop for a deep breath before he started to speak. "There was a power blackout at the construction site of a high tech research facility in West Texas. Now, everything that goes into that area disappears. At first, repair crews from the local utility went in and didn't come back. Then police went to investigate and they didn't come back. There were FBI, state guard and finally they called us." The General's agitation rose as he went through the story.

"What are we talking about? ... like the Bermuda Triangle?" The Mistress was having trouble believing him but knew the man wasn't a lunatic or a liar.

"At first, we sent a few men who didn't come back then we sent truckloads. Some of our teams returned on foot saying that their vehicles stopped running and radios wouldn't work but that there was nothing there." The General could still tell that the Mistress didn't understand so he continued. "I sent in three recon helicopters that all crashed and fifteen people died. We sent a high altitude spy plane and three more people died. We established a strategic headquarters on the edge of the area and the next day the blackout area doubled in size and no one there has been heard from since. I was on my way there when we lost contact ... Hell, I even sent in a team of guys on bicycles hoping someone could pedal back with first hand info ... They're gone."

"I haven't heard anything about this?" she said with a dubious head tilt.

"Keeping it a secret has been the toughest part. Especially with what's going on across the country."

Mistress Valerie still wasn't sure what to make of all this. She considered herself an expert on human psyche but the General's announcement that he was suddenly leaving everything staggered her. She'd seen men do this kind of thing before but not a man like the General. She looked at him still puzzled.

"You haven't noticed yet!" he said incredulous. "Mistress, haven't you noticed people disappearing?

People you know that are here one day then gone the next?"

"Well, people come and go in my business. There have been world wars, depressions, hurricanes, life goes on. Who's disappearing?" she asked.

"People ... just people from everywhere for no reason." The General was taken aback by the fact that she didn't know and stood up to pace as he explained. "There were a few cases at first but they began to pile up and soon law enforcement recognized an epidemic. In less than three weeks, two million people across the United States vanished from all walks of life with no connection. It's increasing ... Forty five hundred people disappear every hour without a trace. We can't cover it anymore. In months, the North American continent will be uninhabited. I'm supposed to fly out tomorrow for a press conference with the Secretary of State to deny the disappearance of a local TV news crew but the Secretary of State been gone for forty-eight hours."

"Well," the mistress said, breathless from the General's story. "The walls of our establishment have been privy to a lot of political secrets in our time but this is a first. Do you think the secretary of state just took off?"

"I don't know ... All the TV and radio talk shows are going nuts over flying saucers and the Internet has all kinds of stories and pictures of little aliens strapping nude women to tables for experiments. The TV evangelists are saying that this is the 'Rapture' described in the Bible and these people are being taken to heaven. But Mistress, I know some of the missing people personally and I know for a fact that they were going to hell. Anyway ... it doesn't matter. Forty-eight hours is about as long as the Secretary of State can be missing before the world finds out. The general tried to muster up some foxhole humor to fend off a tear building. "Normally, I'd ask my secretary to handle it but she's been missing a week."

The Mistress had seen a lot in her life. She'd spent a year kept by a Jordanian oil baron on a palatial yacht traveling the Mediterranean and Red Sea. She had lived with junkies near Times Square. While some guys dreamt of her putting metal clamps on their genitals, others wanted her to put a baby bonnet on them and diaper them. For the General, it was utter submission that released him. When he looked up at her from the floor his eyes gave her anything she wanted. Now all she saw in those eyes was fear. It was fear from a man who had lived through wars and made it his career. She still wasn't sure what he was talking about but it was scaring her.

"Mistress, do you remember the first time you took me to your dungeon?" the General reminisced.

"Every new submissive starts out the same, bound, naked, spread eagle, gagged," Mistress Valerie said smiling at the memories. "Alone," she added.

"You stood in front of me peeled your panties off and made me wear them." As he spoke his eyes rolled back. "They were so silky and I was so turned on that I came in them. That's a part of me that my wife, my family, my world, my job would never accept. But you accept any part of me ... I know that I could tell you anything. It was like this place was completely sealed in a world of its own... a world where I could live a life I chose." He pulled a stuffed envelope folded in half from his back pocket and handed it to her. "I have something for you."

Mistress Valerie slowly opened the envelope to find two bundles of fifty one-hundred dollar bills. She missed a breath before she looked up at him and asked, "What's this?"

"I've got no one," the General answered. "My kids have grown and moved away. When I'm gone my wife will have all kinds of life insurance and military benefits. It will probably be months before she notices I'm missing as long as the pool guy keeps coming once a week. This is the one place I could be myself no matter what that was. This place was real." The General just stopped talking.

"General ..." The mistress started to speak then stopped. She was going to try and talk him out of leaving but despite her domination she knew she couldn't really make him do anything he didn't want to do. She started over with what she was saying. "If you need a place to go I know some people ..."

"I've got plans," the General assured her. "I'm looking forward to getting away. The hardest part is that I can feel those missing people calling out to me for help. I know they're alive and I can't do anything about it so I'm going to join them."

153

"I guess this is goodbye," the mistress said slowly with a choke, caught off guard by the emotion of the moment.

"Good bye Mistress," he said allowing his eyes to linger and silently ask permission for a final embrace.

"You may hold me," she said with a smile. As they hugged she whispered, "I'm going to miss you."

The General broke the hug and left the room without looking back.

Outside the mansion the rain had stopped. He surveyed the dark night from the porch for a moment. There were no stars but he knew they were out there; the overcast sky had sealed in the darkness. He saw some flashes in the sky like lightning revealing the silhouette of something large and round couched in the clouds. It loomed like the Goodyear blimp concealed in a fog bank. The moment he became aware of the shadow in the clouds it suddenly lit up. Shafts of white lights shot out of large square windows revealing brightly lit rooms and people inside. The edge was traced with small colored twinkling lights. A solid white spotlight fell on the General and hit him like a gust of wind. He felt himself being lifted and knew it was all over.

It didn't bother him so much to fall in battle as it did to fall in battle as a general. During his time in the trenches of several wars he was faced with death many times but now his death meant something different. It meant that the flag had been captured and America had fallen leaving the outlaws and anarchists in charge. With the U.S. Army gone, no one was left. As he floated upward, he could already see North America as an empty desert crossed only by a few bikers and transients left behind because they weren't worth taking.

# Chapter Seven

## Spyder Mike comes to town

In the middle of the Arizona desert at midnight Professor Kroner and the little girl stood looking up at the stars. "You see, my little angel, G.I.Joe isn't coming," he said as he knelt down to her. "He's gone." His face showed genuine concern over the little girl's loss just to mock her.

She coyly looked past him with indifference clutching her Barbie doll tightly and knowing that this grown-up clearly didn't know what he was talking about. He might well have said that there is no Santa Claus when obviously there is. She pointed to one of the flickering lights on the starry horizon which wasn't actually a star but a campfire in the distance. Professor Kroner began studying the distant fire and could hear rowdy laughter drifting over the desert. He could see two men seated around the fire passing a bottle of whiskey back and forth laughing and yelling. They were big burly men with beards and behind them the chrome of two motorcycles in the shadows reflected the flickering campfire.

Spyder Mike and Steven sat around a small fire that lit their campsite. As the desert spread out around them in all directions, their entire campsite was reduced to just another pinpoint of light lost in the starry sky. There was no one else for a hundred miles and the dark horizon merged with the moonless black night so instead of land and sky there was dimensionless darkness. Their rowdy laughing and yelling echoed through the empty void and they could imagine themselves being the only people on the planet. Harley Davidson motorcycles were only part of what they had in common. They were both over three hundred pounds with long curly beards and they both loved to drink. They also shared things missing from their lives like no family and no plans for the future beyond a few motorcycle rallies.

"There's something natural about sitting on the ground drinking around the fire," Steven said as he settled back against a large rock with the hip flask from the saddle bag on his motorcycle. "You know? The whiskey's gotten better but men have been doing this for hundreds of years, better than anything my great grand dad distilled." Steven had been traveling alone for a number of years and didn't need conversation but had come to enjoy the back and forth banter that traveling with Spyder Mike allowed.

"Granddad even got blown up by a bourbon still. Can you

imagine making all the way through World War I just for that? My family back east still has a few bottles of his brew," Steven said taking a swig from the flask.

"Well, somethings haven't changed." Spyder Mike reached into the pocket of the black leather vest he wore over a white tee shirt. He produced a small wad of aluminum foil in a hand tattooed with the name of a woman he left in Ohio. "Mother nature's recipes are still the best," he said smiling. Most of his large face was concealed by curly fluffy beard but when he smiled the hair parted to reveal teeth but no lips. The several grams of psilocybin mushrooms wrapped in the foil were easily enough to keep both of them laughing and hallucinating for nine or ten hours. They had taken some a few days ago when they first bought them from an old bony nervous Hispanic man in El Paso. But now they could relax and enjoy the effect amidst the grandeur of nature away from any city's police department.

"Before you go chomping on those let's get a joint fired up to help deal with the taste," Steven said.

"Sounds like a plan, bubba."

They got comfortable passing the flask and joint back and forth between themselves. Seated against the rocks they were as kings in a throne room laughing and swapping stories of the road. Soon, the mushrooms were divided into two portions which they chewed up and swallowed. "God I hate the way these things taste. Like dogshit!" Steven observed contorting his face beneath his beard.

"That's cause they grow them in shit. But you know it's cowshit not dogshit." Spyder Mike answered.

"Well, the next time I do shrooms, I'm washing them off!"

"Oh no! You can't do that!" Spyder Mike said laughing. "The shit is the part that gives you the buzz!"

"Did you see that?" Steven said with a sudden concerned look at a light on the horizon. "That light?"

"Boy, don't be tugging my spud," Spyder Mike said. "You can't be tripping yet. Now maybe in thirty, forty minutes we'll be seeing lights."

"No man, I'm serious look off to the east. It's one of those UFOs everybody's talking about."

Spyder Mike hadn't known Steven all that long but long enough to know that he wasn't the panicky, UFO type. He'd seen him handle cops, other bikers and a half dozen drunken cowboys. It surprised Spyder Mike to see Steven this way but then off to the east, he could see some kind of brightly lit aircraft coming towards them. Both men stood up and stepped away from the fire to face east but whatever it was vanished. He thought at first it might have been a game warden chopper looking for poachers or INS looking for illegal aliens but realized the craft had made no sound. There was no way a chopper could have disappeared that fast and they would have heard it even at this distance. They started to scan the sky and saw that groups of stars were moving in formation. They formed complex patterns like rows of domino faces carrying a coded message scrolling across the sky. It was like watching the aurora borealis.

In his years of travel, Spyder Mike had never seen any sasquatches, bigfoots, chupa cabras or mothmen but he'd never seen anything to rule them out. All the strange things he had seen on the road made him suspect there were a lot more strange things he hadn't seen. Now, after all the stories on the news and paranoid talk-radio, he was looking at no shit UFOs. They watched the spectacle spellbound when suddenly something large and bright swooped up from behind them causing both men to duck down as it passed quietly overhead like a breeze. It was bigger than a helicopter, round with lit windows all over it and absolutely silent.

They watched the strangely shaped aircraft circle around lighting up the area before it settled on the ground out of sight behind a ridge near their camp. "Well, let's go introduce ourselves," Steven said obviously certain that this vehicle wasn't the I.N.S. or D.E.A. There was something festive about the colored lights reminding Steven of a carnival midway and gave him the same excited feeling he got as a child.

Spyder Mike didn't feel the excitement. Instead, he dug through his backpack and produced a small shotgun. It had both the barrel sawed off and the shoulder stock sawed off so it could be handled like a pistol. The sight of the gun surprised Steven. He wasn't surprised that Spyder Mike had it but that he felt he needed it now. "I'm taking the scatter gun just in case these are the flesh eating, brain sucking, buttfucking kind of aliens," Spyder Mike explained. "I've seen them in the movies." He also dug out a flashlight but it didn't work so he put it back.

They crawled up on to the head high rocks and boulders which stood between them and what had settled in the desert. From this vantage point they had a commanding view of the glowing craft hovering a few feet off the ground. It was disc shaped and had rows of square windows with square shafts of white hot light coming out of them. Colored spotlights shined out of its sides and twinkled on and off lighting up the desert. "You think we're the only people seeing this?" Steven asked surveying the spectacle wide eyed as a child. It dawned on him that there were no people for a hundred miles and no way to know this was really happening.

They both found themselves staring at it like they were daydreaming, the type of daydream you drift totally into. The white light from the craft held their attention leaving their bodies paralyzed. In horror, they found themselves unable to break out of the daydream. Panic overwhelmed each of them but the only physical movements they could make were to widen their eyes. In a split second, Spyder Mike's mind returned to a childhood image of a fly stuck on one of those sticky strips he had seen hanging at a family reunion decades ago. At least the fly could thrash his arms and legs around and shoot the finger at his captors as they walked around him. All he could do was stand there dumbfounded while shadowy silhouettes came stretching towards him from the light. He heard his shotgun fall on the ground.

The light that held their attention became so intense that it solidified into walls and a hazy room around them. Spyder Mike could hear voices in the air but they were muffled so he couldn't understand them. Small gray people scuttling in the haze gathered around Steven and picked him up like ants carrying a bread crust then laid him on a metal examination table on the other side of the room. They moved around the three hundred pound man without fear even though he was many times their size and not physically restrained. For them, he wasn't even real but just a source of consciousness to navigate by. Spyder Mike would stand there and watch them dissect his friend because that's what they wanted.

"I'll kill all you little son-of-a-bitches!" Spyder Mike shouted in his mind creating a brilliant beacon of awareness. His body stood with mute wide eyes as he watched the small gray people gather around Steven's limp body. Their glassy black eyes glinted with intent purpose. They huddled around Steven concealing him from Spyder Mike's view then one of them left the huddle carrying Steven's arm. The being carried away the heavy limb allowing Spyder Mike to see the severed end. It wasn't bleeding but red and meaty like the clean cut of a steak in the butcher shop.

The gruesome spectacle was repeated when two more of the small people carried away a forty pound leg still twitching. Spyder Mike felt himself succumbing to shock as the reality of the situation sank in. There was pain here. He could now almost understand some of the voices in the air and he knew that whatever they were doing they had done it before. The haze cleared as the experience intensified and the people around the table left to reveal Steven's limbless head and torso wriggling there. His eyes were blinking hard and his mouth was opening and closing in dumb silence as he thumped around with stumps that revealed wet, red flesh around a core of bone. Suddenly, the table opened like a trap door and swallowed what was left of Steven then closed back standing ready for the next person to go on it. Dozens of black slanted eyes then turned to Spyder Mike, frozen in the exact same position he was in when he first saw the craft.

One small gray person came forward and curled three long fingers around Spyder Mike's arm as if to lead him to the table. In the middle of this experience beyond his imagination, he felt something familiar wash over him. It was a sensation he had felt somewhere before. A tingle ran up the back of his neck then spread over his head and he could feel the flesh under his scalp crawling like goose bumps in his hair. There was a sound like a strong wind rising in his ears. The psychedelic mushrooms were kicking in.

The high from psychedelic mushrooms is like getting severely tickled to the point of hallucinations and it's a feeling that doesn't stop for hours. His pulse changed gears from pounding with fear to racing shallow beats like a hummingbird. He started to see ultraviolet purple spots in his peripheral vision. For a moment, he even forgot where he was and almost started to smile. Then the alien tugged on his arm breaking the trip. Spyder Mike turned a contemptuous look on the little gray man that was so intense it stopped the being in his tracks and held it still. He felt another tug on his arm.

"No!" Spyder Mike shouted yanking his arm away and sending the little man reeling backwards. Everything stopped. The aliens watching were frozen by what they saw. All the muffled voices that hung in the air stopped. Even the flickering lights on the walls stopped blinking. Spyder Mike looked at his arm which was now free to move then looked up at the aliens who were petrified with terror. He then looked at the table where Steven had been. There weren't many people he cared enough to talk to much less fight for but in the few weeks they'd spent together on the road he and Steven looked out for each other. Now Steven was gone.

The aliens saw Spyder Mike standing still and slowly started creeping up on him. He stood still a few seconds more to let them get closer then he let out a deep animal roar that's only possible for an animal with a large chest cavity to give it a powerful bass resonance. He threw a straight lunge punch into the face of the nearest alien whose gray head collapsed like a melon into a mass of pink jelly. The virtually decapitated body stood for only a split second before it fell like a pile of wet warm noodles. Amped on the mushrooms, Spyder Mike's mind raced trying to relate the texture of the alien head to something he could recognize. He finally decided it was like a Styrofoam skull filled with pepto bismol jelly and covered with a gray orange rind skin.

Chaos erupted around him. Some of the aliens started squealing in panic and fled while others fell to their knees at the sight of an otherwise immortal being destroyed. Disbelief that a mindless puff of psychic energy reflecting their own conscience could physically become a snarling beast capable of ending an infinite life. As they had become real to us we had become real to them. Horror swept over a million minds as they had to deal with a concept that was a fundamental truth of all that is finite and real: death. Amidst the squealing and alarms an alien darted in front of Spyder Mike who snatched its little gray arm and snapped the entire creature like a bullwhip. Its body broke loose and slammed against the wall across the room. The dismembered arm was a perfect weapon for him to start slashing at the small herd of frightened aliens which scattered in all directions as he bellowed and charged.

One of the fleeing aliens broke left and got past Spyder Mike to the other side of the room and slapped a three fingered hand onto a lighted spot on the wall. Spyder Mike threw up his arms in front of his face fully expecting to get vaporized or something but nothing happened. Then he realized the floor was gone from underneath him and he could see the night desert sixty feet below his feet. Like so many comical Saturday morning cartoons he watched as a kid, he had a chance to look up at his captors with a bamboozled look before plummeting to the ground. There was some kind of gravity field or magnetic beam suspending the craft that slowed his fall but he still impacted with a thump that could be felt in the ground for a radius of several feet.

Spyder Mike still wasn't thinking but acting on psilocybin, adrenaline and instinct. Bouncing up on hands and knees, he scrambled away on all fours kicking up dust and gravel. He saw his shotgun lying on the ground and dived onto it rolling up on to one knee with the gun firing. But in a flash and a dusty blast of wind the craft was gone leaving only the echoes of his shouts and shotgun blasts. Peace descended on the starry night and the only movement was three stars of the billions moving in formation from their place in the constellations.

The thought of what just happened was sinking in and it held him there panting with the smoking shotgun hanging in his hand at his side. The psychedelic buzz had been almost completely burned off in the half hour of adrenaline and stress leaving only fatigue. This couldn't be real, there was no point in telling anyone. He looked over at the camp where the two motorcycles were parked. Steven had been real and now he's gone leaving no family or even birth

172

certificate behind to prove he ever existed. There was no proof any of this happened until Spyder Mike saw something lying in the dirt.

The sun had been up for a couple of hours the next morning when Spyder Mike rolled slowly into the small town puzzled by the empty streets and closed stores. His Harley-Davidson motorcycle rumbled along at a low RPM just enough to keep him moving. He could sense a quiet in the air that he couldn't understand. It was some tangible stillness like Christmas morning in the small desert town. Even his motorcycle seemed to hold its engine noise under its breath.

He saw no one as he motored down the main street towards the city hall. He only caught glimpses of faces peeking at him from around corners and between closed shades. The minute he caught their eyes they disappeared. He was used to that reaction from small town folks but for some reason these particular folks were actually making him nervous.  Turning a corner onto a dusty road through the middle of town he could see the stone brick city hall building awash in a mass of noisy people.  Some were shouting, some had crude, handwritten signs and all were angry.  He knew what they were angry about even before he was close enough to read the signs.  They were angry because they were scared, scared for their families, scared for their lives and after what happened to Steven in the desert he didn't blame them.

The crowd that jammed the entrance didn't notice him pull up on his motorcycle.  They continued shouting and waving signs that had quotes like "Sheriff Gonzales Lies" and "Save Our Families".  Spyder Mike was dismayed for not being noticed.  A large burly man on a motorcycle usually gets noticed.  "These people got no clue," he thought surveying the scene for a minute then revving the motor hard a couple of times with a roar that rattled the windows on the building.  The entire crowd fell silent and turned to stare at him. He calmly turned off the motor and got off the bike taking a back pack with him. The crowd parted like the Red Sea before Moses as he walked up the steps to the front door of the building. He didn't waste a look on any of the staring people.

There was a whole new world of chaos inside the building. He pushed through a hallway packed with people being handled by a smattering of uniformed deputies trying to keep order. As he walked he picked up snippets of conversations like, "We're doing all we can ..." and "Please be calm ..." One deputy was trying to shout over the crowd, "If you have complete paperwork for someone who's missing you can get into the line at the desk in the front office!" This was followed by pleas for calm and cooperation. Spyder Mike pushed on through without a look at any of it.

He got into the hallway outside the sheriff's office that seemed to be the focal point of all the activity. People were

175

screaming at officers waving forms, and officers were screaming back. Spyder Mike stood unnoticed for a moment before it became clear that he wouldn't get any attention. He crawled up and stood on a desk, his bulk looming high over the crowd. Slowly, people began to notice him standing there like a giant and the room got quiet. A scrawny deputy called the sheriff out from his office. Sheriff Gonzalez, a broad shouldered Hispanic vaquero stepped out of his office and locked eyes on spider Mike who didn't flinch.

"Son, we're kinda busy here, you need to get off the furniture," the sheriff said up to Spyder Mike. Sheriff Gonzales was used to frontier justice and wasn't unnerved easily. "You got some kind of problem?" the sheriff asked.

"Yes sir, I need to report a UFO," Spyder Mike said it like a threat and he wasn't about to disappear into the rabble. The declaration brought a gasp from the crowd. "... saw it about a hundred and ten miles west in the desert.

They took my buddy and I want you to do something about it."

"Son, people see all kinds of things in the desert ..." The sheriff started to speak but was drowned out by rising boos, hisses and cat calls. He silenced them with a screech from a chrome coach's whistle that hung around his neck and continued in a louder voice. "You people with your flying saucers, we can't help you without any proof. You don't have any pictures or anything to prove any of this is really happening!"

"The crowd started heckling and shouting again but Spyder Mike stopped it abruptly when he shouted, "I got proof!" All eyes were upon him.

The sheriff stood firm eyeing him suspiciously. "You got proof?" The crowd held its breath as Spyder Mike and the sheriff maintained their stare down. "Okay jeffe, let's see your proof."

Spyder Mike calmly removed his back pack from his shoulder and pulled from it the dismembered arm that he tore off the small gray alien. He held it over his head like a trophy with the limp three fingered hand on one end and tattered flesh at the other. The crowd erupted into chaos as people started screaming at the sight of their nightmare made flesh, made real. Some had been so traumatized by alien visions that they fell to their knees and wept when they saw that it was real.

"That's it!" the sheriff shouted over the erupting melee. "Clear this room, grab that biker son of a bitch and bring him to my office! Denton! Call the FBI and tell them that we need some more of those government assholes down here! Now!"

Professor Kroner had been watching the incident from the desert with the five year old Cassie at his side. He stood dumbfounded that an infinite intelligence could be tripped up by the infinite imagination of a little girl.

Suddenly the small child's hand snatched the glasses from his face and his multidimensional world went blurry. He thrashed around in panic, trapped in the image that he had created to torment her.

"Now you can't see, now you can't see!" the little girl shouted gleefully running around him in a tight circle waving his glasses. She stopped long enough to deliberately kick him in the ankle causing him to yelp and waver as he picked up his foot to cradle the kicked ankle. Stepping over to his other leg, she kicked him in that ankle sending him to the ground. As he fell, the little girl hopped up onto his stomach then jumped up and stomped down as hard as she could with both feet knocking the wind out of him.

The Professor lay there gasping before struggling up onto his hands and knees. The moppet scampered off giggling and waving the glasses over her head as the professor began crawling blindly across the desert. "It's not over yet!" he shouted into the fog desperately. "It is not over!" He thought he was shouting at the receding silhouette of the vanishing little girl but it was a group of human men dressed in black marching towards him with unflinching resolve.

# Chapter Eight

## Battle of the Brink

The desert of west Texas reminded Staff Sergeant Becker of the deserts of Arizona, Iraq, Afghanistan and Africa. Even though he'd never been here before, the desert environment was the last familiar element of life he had to cling to. Everything else was gone. When Becker joined the Army ten years ago, his whole world was reduced to the contents of a foot locker that could be replaced by placing a requisition form but now it was the outside world that was missing parts. A group of his friends that were in the first Gulf War with him went AWOL for no reason, everyone above him in the chain of command had been replaced from the top down over night and now he was leading a team of strangers from all branches of the military into an empty desert. The uniform dress and the syncopate step gave them a mechanical look that concealed an entire cosmos of humanity in each of them.

He didn't know why this deployment should be so different but it was like his life had suddenly opened a new chapter where everything started without telling him the whole story. He still wasn't sure that this entire exercise wasn't some type of military psychological test especially after the way the Navy captain giving the briefings for this mission had just disappeared after lunch along with two

Lieutenants that went to look for him. The team had been sitting silently in the empty briefing room for a half hour before an Army major poked his head in and realized something had gone wrong. Almost in a panic, the Major continued the briefings and hustled through some maps of the area before confessing, "Gentlemen, an unknown group has set up an energy field that seems to dampen electricity and everyone sent to investigate disappears. You will march to the site and disable that field, Staff Sergeant Becker will lead." Becker was dumbfounded by the bizarre briefing and even more dumbfounded by his seemingly random selection to be the mission leader.

Twelve hours later, as he lead the team down an empty dirt road in the desert looking for 'a saucer-shaped structure', Becker felt like he had the same confused look on his face that he had when he got this assignment. The men in his command were all suspicious of him as if he knew what was going on and had something to do with the disappearance of the others.  In the brief time they got to know each other they found that the only thing they had in common was hand-to-hand combat experience.  It almost explained the strange selection of weapons, the standard automatic rifle and side arm, a nightstick, a bowie knife, grenades and four pounds of plastic explosives.  Then they were told they would be given a drug made from psychedelic mushrooms.  The circumstances were so unreal he thought this had to be some kind of test.

They had been ordered to remain silent while they marched, and to use only hand gestures to communicate. His watch stopped and the radios went dead as expected isolating him with his thoughts as they marched with clockwork rhythm down the dirt road.  In the past, when he faced danger, he would think of how proud his family in Idaho was and that they were thinking of him even when they weren't allowed to know where he was.  He had no brothers or sisters so once his aging parents were gone he would be alone with his career. Now he was a stranger among strangers with all of his friends, his family and even the direction of his life so far away that he had to wonder who he himself was.

He knew lots of career army guys who did have families back home somewhere else and who raised happy, healthy kids. They all finished their tours with honor and went back home playing baseball with those kids on weekends. He would never regret his service to his country but he still felt like he would never know what he missed. Becker could easily imagine meeting some smart, beautiful woman to build a life with but he knew she could never leave his dream world. He could lose himself in that idea, escaping the emptiness of his surroundings. Friends that he once called 'animals' now sent him pictures of their new toddlers while he hadn't even held a woman in his arms for more than three years. He wanted to go on composing the perfect woman in his head but his mission started to overshadow everything like the growing silver structure he noticed on the horizon.

They passed a dozen bicycles lying on the side of the road but he couldn't look at them. It would break his forward marching gaze and remind him of the last team that was sent here by the generals and politicians. At least, they had bicycles to ride before they vanished. They were probably outfitted very similarly to himself but without orders to take a dose of hallucinogen. He thought he saw a little girl standing next to the bicycles for a moment but he blinked hard a couple of times and his vision cleared revealing wavy lines of heat over the dirt. It was like the world itself was quivering under the weight of his thoughts.

A ten-foot tall chain link fence topped with coiled razor wire completely surrounded the site in a perfect circle seven miles across. They marched in two rows of five through the open gate and Becker stole a glance down the fence line. The fence had no corners but was so long that it curved around just before it would disappear over the horizon. It looked like the fence pinched off a part of the planet with the giant silver saucer at its center. The time had come so he stopped the team's rhythmic marching by raising his fist over his head and pulled a small plastic squirt bottle out of a pocket on the sleeve of his black jumpsuit. The rest of the team followed the example and each placed three drops of bitter liquid in the bottom of their mouth under the tongue as they had been ordered.

There were people that would give up their careers over the Army's use of chemicals on soldiers but for Becker 'go pills' and smallpox vaccines were just part of the job. For all he knew, this whole scenario was a training exercise and the drops were a harmless placebo that was part of some experiment. The liquid did leave some weird tingle in his mouth like an anesthetic that didn't seem right. If it was some hallucinogen he would have to stay focused on the awareness that his senses could lie to him and he might not be able to tell what was real. He could only hope that the members of his heavily armed team could control themselves as well. As his mind reeled with possibilities he knew that someone outside of himself knew the truth about the drug they took and someone outside of them knew why they were told to take it. There was still somebody else outside of everybody that not only knew what he took, knew why he took it and knew why there was an immense silver disk at the center of this area.

They continued their march down the dusty road past abandoned construction vehicles. The silver disc structure continued to get larger as they got closer so eventually they could grasp its true size. It was almost four hundred feet across and three stories high. There was nothing particularly threatening about it but when they got to within a half mile they could see that it was actually floating five feet off the ground with no visible means of support. Without breaking his march, Becker's eyes desperately scanned for something holding this immense thing off the ground knowing there had to be some support columns under it that he couldn't yet see. He still didn't know what he was looking at but he now knew it was real and not some Army exercise.

He noticed jagged colored lines shaking in his peripheral vision that vanished like floaters when he tried to focus on them. Suddenly his scalp began to crawl and tingle like a swarm of ants was spreading over his head through his hair. He fought the urge to whip off his cap searching for ants with the recognition that the drugs were real and these were just the first jittery effects. He wondered what it was doing to the other guys on the team and a moment of paranoia swept over him realizing that all he really knew about them was that they were all highly trained killers. Three circular lights flashed across his field of vision in formation through the sky but they moved so fast, like sunlight reflected from a mirror, that he knew they were just visual distortions and there would be more to come.

They stopped just twenty yards from the giant disk. It had the classic flying saucer shape that he'd seen in cartoons, comics and movies since childhood but that was the only familiar thing about this structure. There were no seams, rivets or screws anywhere on it. As impossible as it seemed, it looked to be machined from one huge piece of metal and reminded him of an old 1950's science fiction movie called, "The Day the Earth Stood Still." In the movie, a friendly alien in a flying saucer lands on earth in front of the White House to introduce himself and a nervous infantryman guns him down causing the alien to unleash GORT, the killer robot. Becker had to shake the idea that he could be the one to bring GORT down on the human race and reproached himself for wasting his consciousness on old sci-fi flying saucers during the height of a tense mission.

He signaled the younger, Hispanic man standing to his right, a man he only knew as "Navy Ensign Gomez" and the two of them approached the saucer while the rest of the team watched. It called out for him to touch it and he knew that there was no way anything this impossible would be normal to the touch. He gingerly reached out to touch its surface and could sense the team watching tensely expecting him to get vaporized or frozen upon contact. But like a soap bubble, it drifted away weightlessly under his fingertips. This vast construction moved like a balloon almost eight inches off center of the circular collider site. It was so large that when it moved it created the illusion that the structure was motionless and the earth was moving under it. Becker had to steady himself as the saucer responded to his touch with just the unimaginable reaction that he would imagine.

The shiny brushed metal surface held his gaze and he couldn't pull his attention away from it. In horror, he

191

realized that his mind was frozen like he was occupied by an intense daydream and unable to move. His daydream was of a bright white light bathing him and Gomez. The feeling was somehow familiar and reminded him of once being asleep and not being able to wake up even though he knew he was sleeping. He had no control over his body like a paralysis but could only focus his strength just enough to move his eyes sideways and see Ensign Gomez standing like a statue.

The rest of the team a few yards down the road were hypnotized by what they saw. It was a bright white light they could see even under the midday desert sun. They were also paralyzed except for twitches, nervous tics and sweats brought on as the psychedelic drugs started to affect them. But then the light was gone along with Becker and Ensign Gomez. The giant craft sat in the middle of science's most ambitious project mocking humanity, then reached out to seize the minds of the entire team and torture them.  Each one felt something different and horrible on personal and physical levels.  One man felt a live eel in his stomach writhing around trying to squirm farther down into his intestines while another felt like he was falling face forward through the air with his hands tied behind his back.  One man realized that his heart was missing every fourth beat then suddenly it started missing two out of four beats and he had to focus all his fear on just trying to keep his heart beating regularly to survive.  It went on for thousands of years while they stood there motionless.

Becker and Gomez were daydreaming that they had been led away by a group of children when they suddenly realized that they weren't in the desert anymore.  They had only taken two sleepy half steps but now they were in a brightly lit room that was so foggy they could barely make out examination tables and computer consoles around them.  The fog cleared as Becker understood that he had been taken inside the saucer and he could see that the computer screens were just glass panels covered with glowing lights and symbols. The two examination tables were only two feet off the ground and made of the same metal that the walls, ceilings and outside of the saucer were made of. He realized as the details of his surroundings assembled themselves that the group of children staring at them was really a group of small gray people with skinny arms and legs, large heads and shiny black almond eyes.

Becker stood staring at the little gray people for an eternal moment and they stood staring back. Their eyes locked with his and he spent that moment desperately searching those glassy black almond eyes for any sign of life. As deep as he looked he didn't even see the life he saw in the eyes of a snake or insect, just mindless intelligence. He stared at the detail of an alien's face trying to find something that he could reconcile with any person or animal he had ever seen before but the sound of a rising wind was making it difficult to concentrate. He was having trouble seeing through the jagged lines in his vision and knew that the full effects of the drugs were raging in his mind. A bead of sweat rolled down on his ear and he reflexively wiped it away as he stood then suddenly realized that he was free to move. Gomez turned his head to look at the Becker's move and realized at turning his head that he was also free. The aliens grew wide eyed.

"Don't move. We are going to return your people to you. Just stand still," a reassuring voice drifted in the air as one of the creatures stepped forward with some strange tool that looked like a toy jackhammer. "It's okay. It'll be all right." Despite the soothing voices, something still seemed sinister as if thoughts of ulterior motives were leaking through the voices. The small gray man was trying to look cute walking on the small bare feet of a child and cocking his head to the side like a puppy as he looked up into Gomez's eyes. But then he walked behind Gomez with the device and pointed it at the back of his head. Something about the device gave Becker the images of severed human limbs falling to the floor and piles of human torsos still alive squirming without arms and legs.

Becker saw the device approaching the man's neck and realized that this was his mission. He leapt over and kicked the device out of the alien's hand sending it to smash a glass control panel in a shower of sparks. All of his self doubt and confusion vanished as he drew his rifle and shouted, "Take them out!" Becker and Gomez both began to spray the room with machinegun fire chopping the grey people into fleshy pink chunks that continued to thrash around as they fell on the floor. Bullets crashed through computer screens causing more sparks and setting fires. Weird electronic sirens went off like inhuman screams not just on this ship but on invisible ships all over the world and across dimensions.

There was a surrealistic feel to the act of Becker pulling the trigger like he had never experienced. He wasn't wearing a flak jacket. He wasn't crouched behind crumbling brick of a burned-out building. He was gunning down unarmed, naked, sexless creatures. But as their bodies exploded releasing their lives he could taste their thoughts and saw their agenda. Real and unreal were simply dependent on which way the mirror faced. They would decide what was real to a world that didn't know what real was. We imagined them now they would imagine us. Becker couldn't let that happen.

Gomez charged after two that escaped through a round open doorway into the hall where he surprised more fleeing aliens and instantly pulped them with a barrage of bullets. He rampaged off through the halls yelling like a madman indiscriminately firing at anything that moved or had flashing lights on it.

Becker was left standing alone amongst the settling dust, smoke and twitching remains as Gomez pursued the aliens like a lion after a herd of zebras. "Don't these aliens have ray guns?" Becker thought. A bright hot light flashed past his face and exploded on the wall behind him. He turned to find an alien struggling to hold up a ray gun like a child unsteadily holding a firearm. The alien struggled with the unfamiliar grip trying to relocate the controls and fire it again but the concept of a weapon had little meaning in a world of immortals. Becker drew his pistol and shot the alien in the head blasting away everything from the eyes up. The plastic ray gun clattered to the metal floor as the small being stumbled around spilling dark pink blood and some black brain organs from its open head with one of its big eyes hanging out on a nerve. It stumbled toward Becker clutching at what was coming out of its head chattering like a squirrel, then fell face down on the floor.

Becker stood there frozen with his weapon still drawn on the lifeless body aiming through jagged lines in his vision. The weapon that the alien had dropped did look like an oversize toy made out of red plastic and even had a decorative yellow lightning bolt down the barrel. The UFOs, the aliens and everything about this, were images from things that weren't real. He couldn't move until his pistol started shaking and that shake began to move up his arm and became more violent. His shaking weakened his knees until he leaned against a wall and slumped to the ground seeing the entire ship as a single sealed piece of metal with no way in or out. The voices were telling him that he would run out of bullets and since there was no water he would simply die in a few days. His heart was fluttering, he couldn't fight. All he could do was lay against the wall sweating and trembling at his alien surroundings as voices told him that he would never leave.

In the roar that was blowing through his mind he could hear sirens and alarms going off spreading panic across the ship and across millions of small gray minds in other places. Above it all, Gomez was bellowing like a bull elephant as he spread terror and death down hallways of the immortal. The details of everything around him were so sharp and clear that he was locked into their world like a malignancy. Gomez had them on the run and even the all-knowing voices couldn't stop him. Becker was buoyed up by the image of Gomez running rampant over their abductors and knew then that these people could be beaten. Becker also knew that he would finish this and go on to find a smart beautiful woman to start a family with. That's what he was fighting for. Suddenly, the idea of missing civilians came to his mind and he realized that some of them might be here.

Gomez was also stopped cold as he picked up the thought from the ship that helpless civilians could be around the corner. He couldn't be charging around shooting everything that moved. The smoke began to clear and quiet descended as Gomez stood in the hallway wondering what to do. Small gray heads with large curious black eyes peered around the corner cautiously to see what had stopped the raging beast. After a moment of fighting the psychedelic buzz blowing through his ears, Gomez saw the aliens looking at him and he knew exactly what to do. He drew his night stick like a sword wielding it over his head and whooped like a banshee as he renewed his charge down the hall. He began smashing panels and swinging his club at the scattering little beings that chattered and squealed as they fled before him.

Becker made his way cautiously down the hallway in the opposite direction of Gomez. His mind was being bombarded by a torrent of unrelated thoughts. He saw flashes of this saucer shaped ship all over the world at once as well as far beyond the orbit of Pluto. Everything centered on an image of the giant saucer perched on a high tower looking out over a vast neon city with no horizon. Small rooms within the saucer of different shapes flew around the country taunting farmers, truckers and other individuals separated from humanity by time, distance or

201

state of mind.  He found an opening to another room on his left which he entered with military trained stealth.

The room was white, round, and featureless but in the center he saw something that held him still with his mouth open.  On a low flat table in the middle of the room was a beautiful nude woman laid on her back with her arms at her side as if she was arranged for display.  He couldn't move.  In the moment that he was staring, he found himself almost drifting back into a paralyzing daydream and recognized the dream state as how he had first been trapped here.  The adrenaline rush of the drugs blowing through his head along with the sounds of panic and alarm helped him shake the dream and he slowly approached the woman.

She was about five foot eight and so averagely proportioned that she was perfect.  Her white skin was chilled taut from contact with the metal surface and her breasts pointed straight up.  Her long black hair fell in unkempt curls at her shoulders and her delicate face looked not like someone sleeping but someone frozen in time. He sensed a name: Cassie.

His spell was broken when someone put a deliberate thought in his head. It was again the image of the ship as a sealed single piece of metal. If they ever wanted to leave, Gomez would have to stop chasing people with his club and they would both have to cooperate. Becker gave the thought his attention and a hush fell over the ship along with all the places it existed. Even Gomez stopped to listen telepathically.

"We are leaving!" Becker thought loudly and clearly. He slipped his arms under the woman and lifted her off the table which seemed to start her breathing and bring warmth to her body. As he carried her away, his eyes were transfixed on her beautiful face and he didn't hear the dozens of voices in his head telling him that there was no way off the ship. The entire world was in his arms as he rushed into the hallway to gently lay her down on the floor where she stirred slightly but continued to sleep. "We are leaving right now!" He shouted mentally and verbally. His thoughts could be heard all through the ship and upon hearing them Gomez turned around and began retracing his path of destruction back to meet up with Becker. The voices in the air became almost panicky as they tried to convince him that they were trapped. Then Becker reached into a pocket on his belt and pulled out a four pound brick of the army's latest plastic explosive. He could tell by the shape and slope of the ceiling that it was part of the outer hull.

The thought of setting off an explosion in this structure started more alarms and shouting. The giant saucer had been built upon a tower on their main reactor in the middle of a vast electric city. It would cause such a horrendous dimensional reaction that it would reach into every corner of their infinite world. The most frightening thing about humans was the fact that they could live so calmly day in and day out with the power to vaporize an entire city. Death was a life long companion for a mortal but for an immortal it was an unimaginable abyss from which nothing returned. An air raid siren began to sound over the city and panicked gray masses began to flee knowing that there was no escape but hoping to add a split second more to their lives before the impending conflagration was to consume them.

Becker peeled back the plastic cover from the brick of explosive and there was a flash of white light. They found themselves back in the desert outside the giant saucer. Instantly, the lights on all the personal radios came on and were alive with military chatter. The rest of the team had been standing there with weapons drawn since the moment Becker and Gomez had vanished and were startled into firing by the flash. Amongst the firing and shouting, he heard staticky messages over the radio, "Enemy perimeter compromised! Airstrike inbound, airstrike inbound!"

But there was another flash and Becker looked up just in time to see the immense round structure vanish. It didn't fly away, get small or glow; it simply blinked out of existence. It disappeared so fast that it left a vacuum in the air that it occupied which hung for an imperceptible split second before collapsing with a blast of wind that knocked everyone to the ground with a spray of dirt and gravel.

Becker fell on top of Cassie and shielded her from the wind. When the wind passed, he slowly looked up through the settling dust to see something in the clear desert sky that held him in awe. Other people were getting to their feet wandering what they had been shooting at, shouting at or been scared of. But Becker was still transfixed, seeing something that no one else saw, a vast scar of black night torn in the blue sky. There were all kinds of strangely shaped UFOs flying into the hole in the sky. They looked like fireflies racing into a strip of night closing up like a healing wound then disappearing completely into a blue sunny afternoon.

Only Becker had seen the spectacle in the sky and stared upward as everyone else started to get up and dust themselves off. A second blast of wind and a sound like an explosion knocked them all down again as a formation of jet fighters burst over the horizon just fifty feet over their heads traveling at supersonic speed. The jets tore a path across the empty desert not knowing what they were looking for and not finding anything. When they disappeared over the opposite horizon the dust began to settle again and Becker cautiously stood up blinking hard looking into the cloudless sky at nothing. His bewildered team surrounded him in the middle of the desert and in the seconds that followed, the rinse of time made the vivid image of the impossibly immense craft less real and more dreamlike. In a few minutes, they could barely believe it actually happened. The only proof that anything happened was a beautiful nude woman laid out on the hard dirt. As she began to stir, he knelt over her.

Cassie had been having another nightmare that she was back at her old college and it had been taken over by little gray aliens chasing her up and down endless hallways. They had just caught her, stripped her clothes off and were doing terrible things to her body when a broad shouldered sweaty army soldier dressed in tattered fatigues kicked his way in with a machine gun to rescue her. In her dream, she was not only experiencing the dream as herself but she was also outside her body and could watch the events like an observer. She could even become the soldier and experience it through his consciousness. The full sunlight falling on her face woke her and she began to squirm at the feeling of her bare skin against the dirt. At the same time she realized she was naked she realized that there was a man kneeling over her. While she struggled to wake up she covered her breasts and crotch with her hands wondering who these people were.

Becker realized she was naked in front of him and his team. He could hear radio messages on the walkie talkies that evac choppers were on their way. Soon there would be people all over this area. He got up and started emptying the pockets of his jump suit then unzipped himself out of it.

Cassie was fully awake now and even though she didn't know where she was or who these men in black were, she didn't feel threatened. Their sandy haired leader with the pale blue eyes was unzipping his suit to give to her. As he took it off, he revealed black gym shorts and a black tank top showing off his military physique. She looked around the empty desert and saw no UFOs, aliens or any sign of any of the things she had been dreaming of. All the things that had brought fear to her life were gone including the scary professor from her college days. There were only blue skies and simple honest dirt. She could actually smile

209

at the feeling of the sun on her face.  It was like the first time she felt that feeling since so long ago before the world had broken her.  There was something else strange; it was the feeling of her soft hair on her shoulders.  At work she wore her hair up in a bun and at home she wore it pulled back.  Even when she slept it was tied in a pony tail.  Now it was free.

Becker was still kneeling next to her in awe and reverently handed her the folded suit.  He averted his eyes while she slipped into it but when he looked at her again, the cute way it oversized her and the fact that it had his name embroidered on it took his breath away.  He had to know this woman.

They were interrupted by someone shouting and running towards them with flailing arms and kicking up a dust trail.  It obviously wasn't anyone from the military but a civilian trying desperately to get their attention.

"They're here!" he shouted. "They're here and they're all around us." As the ungainly figure came running at them they could see that he was waving a roll of toilet paper. The team stopped to watch as he came running up. "You must be from the army. Thank God! My name is Walter Smith." Walter was huffing the words to Becker between spells of panting. "Aliens have landed! They're in a giant flying saucer; they just left, probably for Washington DC. We can still catch them!"

"I think everything is under control sir," Becker said calmly. "There aren't any aliens here now but we'll be glad to take your report."

"You can't just take a report!" Walter Smith was incredulous at Becker's apparent indifference to the impending alien invasion. "These things can look like anybody. I've seen them!" Verbalizing what he had seen for the first time made Walter's mind reel. "They could assume our identities. They could be among us!" A panicked look crossed his face. "Mr. Wilmington!" he gasped with a sudden realization.

"What?" Becker asked while trying to think of a way to politely shove this guy off to be debriefed. "Who's Wilmington?"

"Mr. Wilmington is the CEO and owner of the Midwest distributorship of SMS." Walter's story began to take on a life of its own as he told it. "SMS is Supply Management Services and our boss Mr. Wilmington has been acting strange lately!" Walter stopped talking for a moment to compose the rest of the story. "The trade show in Vegas ... He hasn't been the same since. That's where they got to him. Oh my God! His secretary must be one of them too! They've both been assimilated."

"Assimilated?" Becker was trying not to get pulled into the story but it was intensifying. Cassie and the team gathered around Walter to listen in.

"Yeah, assimilated. That's what aliens call it when they erase your mind and steal your body." Walter Smith seemed to know all about aliens.

"Well sir," Becker interrupted him as a small convoy of green army jeeps and trucks pulled up. "We need to hear all about 'alien assimilations' so I'm going to have one of these men drive you back to H.Q." He waved one of the men driving a jeep and gestured for him to come. "Now you go with this man and he'll take care of you."

Walter was about to walk away but stopped to ask Becker in a low voice, "Has he been checked out? You know they can assume any identity."

Becker looked over at the driver of the jeep and assured Walter, "Yeah he's okay. We've all been checked out."

"Well that's good." Walter said resolutely. "We're going to teach those little bastards to mess with the U.S. of A."

"Yes sir," With that, Becker professionally directed Walter Smith off to the waiting jeep. As he watched it drive away, he noticed a few other people scattered around the desert wandering aimlessly.

Gomez saw what Becker was looking at and said, "It looks like just a few dozen of the missing civvies were left here. We may not find the thousands of others that disappeared."

"They're all back home." Cassie said from behind startling them with her voice. "They were never really gone." She could see the skepticism in their faces and answered it. "I don't know how I know that, I just do."

Becker had to smile at her for a moment. She spoke with a confident awareness that he found powerfully attractive. He finally broke his trance and turned to Gomez. "Gomez, go grab a couple of guys with a jeep and start rounding up the civilians, radio H.Q. for a debriefing location." When he turned back to Cassie he found her returning the smile he had given her. Again they were tangled in each others eyes.

An older sharply dressed gentleman in slacks and a knit sweater over a dress shirt and tie walked up to them and interrupted the moment. His platinum hair and air of authority struck recognition in Becker's mind.

"General Van DeMeer is that you?" Becker had rarely seen any of the top brass in casual clothes much less one of the army's highest ranking officers. "General?" he asked.

"Yes soldier, it's me." The general spoke like a loving father instead of a military leader. He simply stood there waiting for Becker to react.

"Well sir, I'll radio a chopper for you ..."

"No that won't be necessary," the General declined sweetly.

"But sir," he was confused by the General's relaxed response and wasn't sure what to make of it. "They're going to need you to meet with them at H.Q. There's going to be debriefings."

"Not for me, son. Not for me." With that, the smiling man turned and began to walk away into the desert.

# Chapter Nine

## Epilogue

"I think you got everything!" Tina's shrill shout echoed against the floor and ceiling of the empty apartment. Through the open front door, she watched Cassie and Becker tying down furniture in the back of Cassie's new pick-up truck. Tina still could not believe that Cassie had sold her Jaguar sports car, much less, sold it to buy the little blue truck. The shiny new truck was cute but it just didn't seem like Cassie's style. Of course, everything that Cassie did lately was surprising Tina more and more.

Cassie finished tying ropes down in the bed of the truck securing her furnishings and left Becker to test and tighten them. She went back into the apartment where Tina caught her.

"Hey Cassie, I think that's the last of it." Tina had been walking around the empty apartment checking closets and drawers. "I can't believe you're moving out. You've lived here as long as I've known you."

"Yeah, well, I guess I've been due for a change." Cassie looked wistfully around the empty room.

"Well 'a change' maybe but you've changed everything since you met Becker Beefcake out there." Tina motioned to Becker out at work in the bed of the truck. "Look at you. I don't think I've ever seen you with your hair down even in a swimming pool. Now, you hair is around your shoulders, you're wearing blue jeans and this sexy halter top. You're not wearing a bra, are you?" Tina hooked the front of Cassie's tank top shirt with her forefinger and pulled out so she could look down into it.

"Hey!" Cassie slapped Tina's hand away. "It has an insert thing built into it. It doesn't need a bra. As far as everything else I just decided it was time for a change. Being a bitch was taking a tremendous amount of energy. Once I began to relax things started looking up."

"I think it has to do more with the lieutenant's military monkey love," Tina countered. "Man, that guy has shoulders that don't stop. I bet he's got something in his pants that won't stop either."

"I'm sure he'd be flattered to hear you say that." Cassie's flushing smile revealed that Tina's comment had hit close to the mark.

"Okay ladies, the final load looks secure," Becker crashed into their intimate moment unaware that he was the

219

target of the covert looks that finished Cassie's and Tina's conversation. "Whenever you're ready, babe." He indicated to Cassie that they were ready to go.

Tina took that moment to grab and hug Cassie. "I'm going to miss you so much."

"Easy girlfriend, I'm only moving an hour away. We can still party together. Now that I cut back on the job we'll probably see more of each other." Cassie broke the hug to look into Tina's eyes.

"I know it was hard losing all those properties when that big SMS deal collapsed but you were pushing yourself way too hard," Tina said then turned to Becker, "You wouldn't believe what a workaholic this woman was just two months ago!"

"Oh you'd be surprised what I'd believe about her." Becker smiled and kissed Cassie on the cheek then said, "I'm going to make one more check around. I'll meet you at the truck." Becker walked off leaving the ladies to admire his bottom as he walked away.

"Cass, you gotta find me one of those," Tina said longingly after Becker.

"Well, I don't know about that but I do have something else for you," Cassie said. "I need someone to take care of that townhouse on Benton Street. If you can pay the monthly property tax you can live there for free."

"No way ..." Tina was aghast. "I can't let you do that! Especially after all those losses you took ... I can't."

"Look, I've still got three other properties paying me rent and Becker's got a pretty cushy civilian job. I know you hate that shit box you're in now ..." Cassie was interrupted by Tina's squeal.

"I don't believe this!" Tina said hugging Cassie again. "I always loved that place, I can't believe it. Are you sure? Are you really sure?"

"You have to believe it because I'm really sure." Cassie said laughing and mocking Tina's excitement.

"But!"

Cassie interrupted Tina's protest then said. "It's all about what you believe. Start packing tonight, I'll call you next week with the arrangements."

"Oh my God ..." Tina was hugging Cassie again tilting her head in a way that would prevent a tear from rolling from her eye. A short beep from the horn of the truck reminded them Becker was waiting. They broke their embrace once more, locked the front door of the apartment and left to get in their separate cars.

Cassie got into the truck next to Becker who was in the driver's seat. "Say, your friend Tina isn't seeing anyone? Right?" he asked.

"No she's as available as they come. Why do you ask?" Cassie answered.

"I got a friend who's getting out of the Navy in a couple of weeks.  Maybe we could get them together.  I think they'd hit it off.  His name's Gomez."

"I think she'd love that."  Cassie smiled.